A Legal Affair

By Alex Strong

A Legal Affair

Cover Art © fotolia/musicman80/Viorel Sima
Cover design by J.P. Irons

ISBN: 978-0-9964709-4-0

I dedicate this book to all the authors who made me want to be one.

One

Elle stood near the poolside in her father's lavish backyard, keeping an eye on her four-year-old son as she chatted with another guest.

"He's so stinking cute," said Cassie as the two of them watched Logan walk up to his grandfather and proudly presented the worm he had just found. Marcus Williams, dressed in khaki slacks and boat shoes, crouched down to eye level with his only grandson.

"What did you find there, Logan?" she heard him ask. Elle could just make out Logan's small voice above the sound of the crowd, but she couldn't catch any of his words. Whatever they were, they caused her father to break into a warm, hearty laugh, and her chest ached knowing that Logan should be having these same moments every day with his own father. But Jason had clearly made his choice.

Marcus pointed to a nearby planter, where Logan gently deposited his new friend before making a beeline for the dessert table.

"Will you excuse me?" Elle asked Cassie, who nodded with a chuckle.

"Not so fast, buddy," she said, blocking Logan's path. "You need to go wash your hands." Logan frowned. "And then you need to eat some real food before you attack the sweets." This time he groaned.

She took his tiny dirty hand in hers and together they walked towards the house. They were a couple steps from the open French doors when a man she didn't recognize came striding through her father's expansive home.

"Can I help you?" she asked, standing between him and the backyard.

"I'm just here for the party," he said and started to step around her, but she moved in his way again.

"I'm sorry," she said, "but this is a private function."

"I know. It's Marcus Williams' annual barbecue. I work for him."

Elle's jaw dropped. His dark hair was looked like it been styled with only gel and his fingers, and the sleeves of his button-down shirt were partially rolled up, revealing tattoos on his forearms. As she took it all in, she wondered exactly what kind of work this man did for her father's prestigious law firm. She met his eyes, and the stranger gave a little smile, clearly pleased to have caught her off guard.

"Wanna see the worm I found?" Logan asked from her side.

"You found a worm?" said the stranger, turning his attention to Logan.

"What?" Elle regained her composure. "No, Sweetie, I don't think he wants to see a dirty earthworm."

"Sure I do," he said as he casually shoved his hands into the pockets of his jeans.

"Well, I'm afraid he needs to wash his hands and eat something," Elle said, feeling the warmth in her cheeks.

The man frowned. "Sorry, little man. Maybe later."

Elle watched him saunter out to the backyard before escorting Logan to the bathroom.

When they came back out, the man was standing with her father, who called her over.

"I would like you to meet Raiden," her father said. "Raiden, this is my daughter, Elle."

"It's a pleasure to meet you, Elle," Raiden said,

extending a hand.

As she accepted it, Elle's eyes fell upon an intricate compass tattoo on his well-defined forearm. She frowned, not really sure why his ink bothered her. She'd never had anything against tattoos before. She lifted her gaze to find Raiden's piercing blue eyes staring right into hers.

She smiled at him as he released her from his strong grip, unable to make her tongue work.

"Wanna see the worm now?" Logan asked, eliciting laughter from everyone but Elle.

"Only if your mom says it's okay," Raiden said, raising an eyebrow at her. She nodded.

Keeping a disapproving eye on the pair, Elle leaned in closer to her father.

"What exactly does Raiden do for you?" she asked in a low voice.

"Raiden Kane happens to be my newest junior associates," he said.

"Junior associate? You mean that man is a lawyer?"

"Yes," Marcus answered with a frown. "Is there something wrong with that?"

"How long has he worked for you?"

"Almost two years now. What's with all the questions?"

"Just curious about the man my son is talking

to," she said with a shrug.

"Oh, really?" her father asked. "Because you wouldn't be the first woman to take notice of him. You should see some of the ladies at the office."

"Don't be ridiculous, Dad." She crossed her arms and ignored the small smile appearing on his face. "I'm just concerned about who my son is hanging around, as you should be." She continued to watch Raiden, who was thoroughly engaged with her son. "Why are we just meeting him now?" she asked. "Why hasn't he come to any of the other barbecues?"

Her father's smile disappeared.

"Something to do with his wife. Well, soon to be ex-wife. He's presently in the midst of a divorce." He cocked his head. "I guess that means he'll be a divorcee soon, just like you."

"I'm not a divorcee," she snapped. Marcus gave a sigh that she ignored as she walked over to where Raiden was crouched down next to Logan, listening to him talk about his Lego sets.

"Hey, you," she said, and they both looked up at her. "You still need to eat something."

"He's adorable," Raiden said as he stood, and she caught a whiff of his woodsy, masculine cologne. It was faint, but it was enough to stir something within her that had been long forgotten.

"Uh, thanks," Elle said with a half-smile as she took a small step back. Why couldn't she function properly around this man? "Let's go, sweetie, before you starve to death."

"Bye," Logan said as he took her hand.

"See you around," Raiden answered.

Elle wondered if he was talking to her or her son.

They grabbed some food from the buffet and found a table to sit at. As they ate, Elle absentmindedly looked around the crowd and caught the eye of Raiden, now flanked by two co-workers who were laughing at something he must have said. He gave her a little smile and she looked back down at her plate, fully aware that she was blushing.

Two hours later she said goodbye to her father and step-mother and poured a cranky Logan into his booster seat. The whole drive from Woodinville to her home in Seattle, she kept thinking about Raiden Kane and wondered why someone she barely knew could rattle her like this.

Later that week, Elle stopped in at her father's firm to drop off some documents she wanted him to go over for her. Sometimes it was handy to have a lawyer in the family.

"This appears pretty straightforward," he said, flipping through the pages. "But I'd like to take it home and look over it better, make sure there aren't any surprise clauses."

"Of course," she said. "I told them I wanted the weekend to think about it."

"Perfect." He slid the file into his bag.

One wall of Marcus' office was glass, and Elle caught sight of Raiden standing outside another associate's office. Her eyes narrowed.

"He doesn't look like a lawyer," she accidentally said out loud.

"Huh?" Her father looked up and he gave a little smile. "Oh, are you talking about Raiden?"

Elle didn't answer.

"What is it that makes you think he doesn't look like a lawyer?" he asked.

"Look at his hair and his tattoos."

Marcus chuckled. "I highly doubt that Raiden is the only person in the legal field who has tattoos. Can you even see any of them now?"

She surveyed Raiden still talking to whoever was in the office. His dark trousers looked tailored, and the trim-cut dress shirt was long-sleeved and cuffed. Not a single tattoo was to be spotted. She frowned.

"What is it exactly that you have against Raiden?"

She spun around and detected a twinkle in her father's eye. "Nothing," she said, perhaps a tad too defensively. "Nothing, I hardly know the man." Elle checked the time. "I should get going. I need to pick up Logan."

She kissed her father on the cheek and walked out, trying to keep her eyes forward as she passed Raiden, but he caught sight of her and gave a smile.

"Elle," he said with a nod. "Nice to see you again."

"Raiden," she said with a curt nod of her own. She thought she heard a chuckle as she continued to the elevator.

Marcus Williams' office was empty when Raiden walked in the following Friday. It was hard to tell if Marcus had simply stepped out or if he had headed home for the evening, so Raiden moved over to the desk. He dropped a file onto it and grabbed a pen and sticky note. As he leaned over to write the message, he saw a line of family photos. They had always been there, but Raiden had never given them much notice until now. He studied one of the pictures of Logan and his mother. Elle's smile was bright and genuine as she wrapped her arms around the little boy, but so far her manner towards Raiden had been nothing but icy. He smirked, remembering how Elle had thought he didn't "belong" in Marcus' home. Raiden wasn't sure what Elle's problem was with him, but he found it amusing that he could ruffle her feathers so easily.

Marcus walked in and Raiden stood up.

"I was just dropping off my notes on the Geurtzen case," Raiden said.

"Anything I should be concerned about?" asked Marcus.

"A couple details. I highlighted them."

"Good." Marcus approached the desk and leafed through the file.

Raiden was almost out the door when Marcus spoke again

"Glad you were finally able to make it to the picnic this year," he said.

"I had a great time. And it was great meeting your family," said Raiden. "That grandson of yours is something else. He cracks me up."

Marcus looked at the same picture Raiden had just been staring at and beamed. "Isn't he amazing? Elle's doing a great job raising him."

"So she's on her own then, I take it?" Raiden asked with caution.

"Logan's father is unfortunately out of the picture, but Elle is doing just fine without him."

Raiden wondered if Elle's problem was with men in general.

"I was wondering if you might help me with

something," Marcus said as he pulled a file out of his bag.

"Of course."

"Only if you have time. I have this document that I need dropped off at Northwest Tutors in Seattle. I could do it myself, it's just that it's in the opposite direction for me…."

"Sure," said Raiden. "What is it?"

"They're partnering with a non-profit and I agreed to go over the contract. I made a couple minor changes in the verbiage, but if they have any questions you should be able to clarify it for them."

"Not a problem. I don't have any more appointments this afternoon."

"Great." Marcus grabbed the note Raiden had never used and scribbled on it. "Here's the address. You'll want to speak with Marielle Peyton. Shouldn't take long."

Raiden took the folder and note from Marcus and gathered what he needed from his desk before heading out. It was late enough in the day that there wasn't much point in coming back to the office.

Traffic on the I-90 floating bridge across Lake Washington was slow, but the summer evening air was warm so Raiden opened the sunroof on his Volvo S60 and turned on The Black Keys. There was nothing to do but enjoy the solitude.

He was whistling "Gold on the Ceiling" as he walked into Northwest Tutors and approached the front desk of the small office. It was vacant, so Raiden waited a few moments, but no one appeared. He peeked around the corner and found an open door to a lit office. He walked up to it and stopped dead in his tracks when he saw Elle sitting on the corner of a desk laughing with another younger female. But the smile disappeared the second she looked up at him.

Two

"What are you doing here?" she asked.

He stared at her, confused. The other girl just looked from him to Elle with a blank expression on her face.

"Your father sent me here. I'm looking for a—" he glanced at the Post-it, "for Marielle. Marielle Peyton."

The girl jumped up and left, closing the door behind her.

"You're joking, right?" asked Elle.

"No, I'm not. I'm assuming you know her?"

"I *am* her. *I'm* Marielle Peyton."

He frowned. "I thought your name was Elle."

"It's short for Marielle," she said.

"And Peyton must be your married name," he said slowly, and she seemed to flinch at his words.

"So what exactly is it that he sent you here for?" she asked with a sigh.

He handed her the folder. "Apparently he was working on a contract for you. He asked me to bring it over and go over any questions you might have."

She took it and plopped it on her desk. "Thank you," she said. "If I have any questions, I'll call my dad."

The smile on Raiden's face was replaced by a frown. "With all due respect, Ms. Peyton, your father asked me to come all this way and go over it with you. I would like to accomplish that task while I'm here."

She rolled her eyes but sat down and opened the file. Raiden made himself comfortable in one of the chairs across from her and took the opportunity to go through some emails on his phone. Suddenly he let out a chuckle, and she looked up.

"What's so funny?"

"I was just thinking that your father must've had a good laugh when I left," he said. She frowned. "Well, obviously he knew exactly who he was sending me to see."

But Elle did not appear to find this funny at all, as she turned her attention back to the contract.

Marcus had left sticky tabs on the pages where he'd made changes, and she was getting through them quickly—until one of the last items.

"I'm confused here," she said. "What's the difference between the original document and what my father wrote?"

Raiden moved around the desk to look at it over her shoulder and wasn't prepared for the warm, intoxicating fragrance that could only be detected in this close proximity to her. It was floral and a little bit spicy and it made him want to bury his mouth in her neck.

"Well?" she asked, cutting into his thoughts.

He cleared his throat, ignoring the desire, and tried to focus on the words. "Um." They were staring right back at him, but he was having trouble reading them.

He stood, distancing himself from her scent, and read them one more time. "The original phrase left too much room for interpretation down the road. Your father's words make it more concise."

"I see." She flipped through the last couple pages while he sat back down, relieved to not be able to smell her anymore. "Should I be concerned?" she asked, closing the file. "Are they trying to screw me over?"

"What makes you say that?"

"Just all the wording that my father changed was closing loopholes. Are they trying to take advantage of me?"

"I don't really know the situation. Your father just mentioned partnering with a non-profit."

Elle sat back in her chair and even brightened a little as she began to speak.

"Northwest Tutors is a for-profit private tutoring company. We connect kids with experts in the subjects they need help with and offer various testing prep courses here in the office. What I've really been wanting to do, though, is connect some of those tutors with more underprivileged students— the ones that could really use a leg up. A few of our tutors have been willing to volunteer some time, but nothing has been real consistent. They have their bills to pay, after all. And now I finally found a not-for-profit group that's willing to partner with us and help with fundraising."

There was a spark in her eye, and Raiden could feel her excitement. He wanted to keep her talking on the subject. "Did you ever try doing any of your own fundraisers?"

"Yes, with minimal success. Most people are reluctant to part with their money for a charitable cause if it's not a tax deduction, and we couldn't offer that. The contract is about making sure most of the money raised in our name goes to this program. Which leads me back to my question. Are they trying to screw me over?"

"I doubt it," he said. "I'm familiar with this organization. They've been around forever and wouldn't be if they were in the business of pulling the rug out from under people. They just have excellent attorneys who are trying to make sure they leave themselves some cushioning in case something goes wrong. Fortunately for you, your father is just as good."

"Thank you," she said with the first genuine smile he had seen from her. "That makes me feel better. I would hate to have to start again. I think my boss might make me scrap the whole idea."

"Why'd you have your father go over it? Surely Northwest Tutors has attorneys they've worked with before."

"They do. But this project has been my baby for the past three years, and I felt more comfortable having my father take a look at it. And it turns out I was right," she said, pointing to one of the highlighted tabs. She stood up and grabbed her bag, clearly heading out for the evening.

"Would you like to grab some dinner?" he asked without thinking.

She looked just as shocked as the moment he told

her he worked for Marcus. She closed her mouth after a pause and glanced at her watch. "I can't. Logan is being dropped off any minute now."

"Bring him then. There's a great pizza place nearby. What kid doesn't love pizza?"

He watched her lips purse. She'd thought Logan would be the perfect excuse not to go. "I guess that might be okay," she said slowly.

"Great. I'll go get us a table while you wait for Logan. You know where Zeke's Pizza is, don't you?" She nodded. "Then I'll see you there in a few."

Elle walked in with Logan and spotted Raiden in a booth. Logan's eyes went big when he realized who was sitting at the table.

"You're the man from Papa's party!" he said.

A huge smile spread across Raiden's face. "Yes, I am. I'm Raiden. How've you been?"

"Good," said Logan as he slid onto the bench across from Raiden, and Elle sat down next to him. "Mommy wouldn't let me take the worm home with me."

Raiden glanced at Elle and chuckled. "I'm sure it was for the best."

A server came over and brought everyone water, reminding Elle that she'd needed to pee for the last hour.

She looked at Logan, who was busy coloring the kid's menu, and said, "C'mon, sweetie, let's go use the restroom."

"But I don't have to go potty," he said without looking up.

"Well Mommy has to go and I need you to come with me."

Logan raised his head. "Why can't I stay here with Raiden?"

She looked at Raiden, hoping he would explain why not, but he just shrugged and said, "It's fine. I think I can handle keeping an eye on him."

Elle frowned, wondering if it was wise. In the end she decided it wasn't worth a tantrum, and besides—her father obviously trusted Raiden or he wouldn't be here.

"Alright, but you have to promise to be good," she said.

Logan grinned. "I will, Mommy."

On the way to the bathroom, Elle wondered why *did* her father send Raiden over? What was he up to?

When she returned to the table, she found Raiden teaching Logan how to play tic tac toe. And Logan was excited because he kept winning.

"Look, Mommy! I'm very good at this game."

"Yes you are," she said, giving Raiden a

knowing smile.

"What can I say?" said Raiden. "The kid's a natural."

The pizza arrived and when Raiden rolled up his sleeves before digging in, Elle saw the edge of the tattoo she had noticed at the party.

"What's the significance of the compass?" she asked before taking a bite.

"It's about finding my direction," he said. "Remembering the path that I'm on."

"And what path is that?"

"Staying out of trouble, helping those that are in trouble."

"And is that something you need reminding of?" she asked with a raised eyebrow.

He laughed. "Not anymore."

"But you did," she said.

He lowered his head in what she thought was more humility than shame. "Once upon a time, yes."

When he didn't explain further, she asked, "Does that have anything to do with how you became a lawyer?"

"Yes."

Elle narrowed her eyes at him. "You are an enigma, Mr. Kane."

His smirk was boyish and even, Elle reluctantly admitted to herself, sexy. "I'm glad you think so."

It had been a long day for the adults, but it was almost to the breaking point for Logan.

"Let's get you home, buddy," Elle said, lifting him out of the booth. He put his head on her shoulder and nuzzled into her neck. She knew he would be asleep before they made it home.

"I'll walk you to your car," Raiden said when they stepped out onto the sidewalk. Happy hour had ended, and for a brief moment the streets were relatively quiet in the lull before the Friday night club-goers started repacking the bars.

"You don't have to," she said.

"I know, but I will. Your hands are full, and I think your father would rather I made sure you got home safely."

"Is that what this is all about?" she asked, heading in the direction of the parking garage she used. "Sucking up to my father."

"I've never felt the need the suck up to Marcus Williams. He's a man who appreciates hard work. I work hard. And I know that if I had a daughter and a gentleman had been to dinner with her, I would expect him to get her safely home. It's the respectable thing to do."

Elle laughed. "So you're a gentleman now."

His stride slowed and she paused with him.

"Have I ever not been a gentleman? Around you at least?"

Her eyes locked onto his. He had a point, but she said nothing and continued on her way.

"Nice vehicle," he said as she strapped Logan into his booster seat.

"Thanks."

"I have the same one. Different color. But I like this lighter shade of gray. It matches your eyes."

Elle felt her cheeks starting to burn but chose not to respond to the subtle compliment. "I never would have pegged you for a Volvo driver."

"They're good cars. Reliable and extremely comfortable," he said. "You obviously trust them enough to drive your son around in one."

She smiled. "Good night, Mr. Kane."

He stepped closer to her. Very close. "Please, call me Raiden," he said as he leaned in, and Elle was sure he was going to kiss her, but then his hand reached around behind her to open the driver's door. She climbed in, cursing the brief disappointment she felt.

"Well, good night Raiden."

"Until next time, Elle," he said with that same boyish smirk and closed the door.

"Elle, dear, what a surprise!" said Marcus when

she walked into his office on Monday.

"I was in the neighborhood and wanted to see if I could take you to lunch," she said. Secretly she had been hoping for a run-in with Raiden, but she wasn't going to admit that to her father. She was having enough trouble admitting it to herself. It bothered her that she hadn't been able to get him off her mind all weekend.

Marcus frowned. "I would much rather be having lunch with you. Unfortunately, I have to head out soon for lunch with a client and I'm still going over these notes for their case."

"I knew it was a long shot," she said, trying to casually glance out through the glass wall.

"Swing by Cassie's desk on your way out and see if she can squeeze something in soon."

"Okay. I'll let you get back to work. Tell Jeannie I said hi."

"Of course. Talk to you soon, sweetie."

Elle stopped to see Cassie who managed to block out an hour for lunch later that week. Elle was pleasantly surprised when Raiden approached.

"Good afternoon," he said, flashing a bright smile.

"Hello," she said. "How was your weekend?"

"Not too bad. What brings you in today?"

"I had an appointment here in Bellevue and

popped by to see if my father was free for lunch, but I guess he already has plans."

Raiden looked at his watch. "I don't suppose you would accept me as a substitute. My treat."

"Well," she said slowly, "if you're buying, then I suppose I'd be a fool to pass that up."

"Great. Let me—"

But just then, a woman came charging down the hall straight for them. A very pregnant woman.

"This is bullshit, Raiden!" she said, slamming a packet on the desk in front of him. "Do you really expect me to agree to this?"

All the brightness faded from Raiden's face, and Elle watched his jaw go tight. "Let's discuss this in my office." He put a hand on her back and guided her down the hall. "Just give me a second," he said over his shoulder to Elle.

"Who is that?" she asked Cassie.

"Oh, that's the ex-wife. Well, soon to be ex. I'm assuming those were the divorce papers in her hand."

Elle felt sick to her stomach. Raiden was in the middle of a divorce with the woman carrying his unborn child. She'd had her share of dead beat dads. Why didn't her own father say something?

"Tell Mr. Kane I had to run," she said and headed for the elevator, leaving behind a perplexed Cassie.

Raiden followed Maureen to the elevator and pressed the button.

"Just have your lawyer contact me next time," he said. "I'd appreciate you not causing any more scenes where I work."

There was a smug look on her face as she stepped through the open doors.

"Or I'll have you charged with harassment." That wiped the grin right off her face, and he smiled at her glowering expression while the doors closed.

He took a deep breath, then walked back to Cassie's desk—she was the only one there.

"Where did Miss Peyton go?" he asked, looking around.

"She had to go," said Cassie.

"Did she say where or why?"

Cassie's shook her head and Raiden frowned.

A can of pens and pencils spilled off Elle's desk and onto the floor as she tried to shove her things into her bag.

"Dammit," she muttered as she stuffed them all back into the can. The foul mood she'd left her father's firm in had only worsened as the day went on. And it was all Raiden's fault. She didn't really know why, because what did it matter to her if he was a scum bag, but he was definitely to blame.

There was a knock at her door. She looked up into the face of Mr. Scum Bag himself, leaning against the door frame with a hand in his pocket.

"What are you doing here?" she asked, blowing a strand of hair out her face.

"You ducked out before we made it to lunch, so I stopped by to see if we could try for dinner instead?"

She stood up and placed the can back on her desk. "I don't think it's a good idea."

"Why not?" he asked, giving her a quizzical look.

She wondered how he could be so cavalier, asking out his boss' daughter while in the middle of a divorce from his pregnant wife.

"You really are something else," she said.

He stepped into the middle of her modest office. "Am I missing something here?"

"Cassie told me who that woman was at your office."

"Ah," he said, crossing his arms. "And you immediately jumped to conclusions, didn't you?"

"I didn't exactly have to jump far," she snorted.

"I don't assume to know your situation any more than you could possibly know mine, but that didn't stop me from wanting to get to know you better. You could have at least extended me the same courtesy."

"The last thing I need right now is more men like

you in my life," she said.

"Men like me, huh?"

She bristled at his comment.

He turned to leave, but then said, "I think, Elle, that you and I both know it wasn't an accident when your father sent me here last week." And he walked out.

Elle slammed her door shut and finished packing up her things. It was true, her father had clearly been up to something. But why would he send a man like Raiden in her direction? Him, of all people.

Elle pressed a button on her steering wheel and gave the voice command to call her father.

"Why did you send Raiden to my office last week?" she asked the second his voice came out of the speakers. His only reply was a hearty chuckle.

"Were you trying to play matchmaker, Dad?"

"Why?" he asked, still laughing. "Is it working?"

"Why would you think I would be interested in someone like Raiden Kane?"

"Because it was obvious you like him," he said. "No matter how much you tried to pretend he was annoying."

"He *is* annoying," said Elle, "and he's a slime ball. I can't believe you would try and set your own daughter up with that man."

"I don't understand. Why do you think that of him?" her father asked. "I think Raiden is a very stand-up gentleman."

"Are you aware that he's leaving his pregnant wife?"

There was an audible sigh from Marcus' end. "The situation isn't what you think, Elle."

"So you do know. What's wrong with you?"

"I told you, it isn't what you think."

"Then enlighten me," she said.

"I don't believe it's my place to share."

"What the hell, Dad?"

"Just talk to him."

"I did talk to him. I told him he could fuck off."

"Marielle Williams!"

The use of her full *maiden* name took her back to the teenage years, and she knew her father wasn't happy.

"Okay, I didn't say it in those exact words," she said.

"Look, Elle," her father's voice was slightly less stern, "you and Logan deserve to be happy, and I saw an opportunity."

"I appreciate you thinking of us, but Logan and I are doing just fine," she said and ended the call before he could reply.

"Have you talked to Raiden yet?" Marcus asked at lunch that Thursday.

"Nope," Elle replied as she laid a napkin across her lap.

"Are you planning to?"

"Don't see the point," she said before taking a drink of water. "May I ask why you care, though?" she said. "Why the sudden desire to play matchmaker?"

"Because I know what it's like to think you can do it all on your own," he said, looking her right in the eye. "I was just as hurt and angry when your mother left us."

Elle wasn't sure that she wanted him to continue. It had always bothered her that her marriage had mirrored that of her parents.

"But Jeannie helped us be a family again. She helped you and me heal."

"Are you saying it's time for me to find Logan a new daddy?" Elle asked snidely.

"Of course not," Marcus said with a scowl. "Is that what you think of Jeannie, that she was just a replacement mother?"

Elle hung her head in shame. Not able to have children of her own, Jeannie had treated Elle like the daughter she would never have, had helped Elle get through her teenage years in a way that her father never would have been able to. Elle loved Jeannie more than her own mother.

"All I'm asking," Marcus continued, "is that you stop working so hard to build these walls around yourself. They're just going to do more harm than good."

"It's hard," she mumbled.

"I know," he said. "Trust me, I know. But just try and think about what I'm saying."

She nodded. Her father's advice made sense, but it was still easier said than done.

"I have to work late tomorrow," Marcus said as they left the restaurant, "but Jeannie says she'll pick Logan up from preschool."

"Sounds good," said Elle. As much as she loved every second with Logan, she always looked forward to his monthly weekend at Nana and Papa's.

"Any big plans?" asked Marcus.

Elle shook her head. "Meeting a friend for happy hour tomorrow, but sadly my weekend will mostly be spent catching up on work. Maybe I can sneak in a bath though. They're much more relaxing when you don't have a four-year-old tapping at the door asking how much longer you're going to be."

Her father laughed. "Ah, the joys of small children. Enjoy it while it lasts, though. Before you know it, he'll be a wonderful adult with children of his own."

Elle thought she saw his eyes mist up, and she hugged him. "I love you, Dad."

"I love you too. See you Sunday afternoon."

Happy hour was almost over, but the bar was even more crowded than when she and Sara had arrived. The Crocodile doubled as a stage venue, and Elle suspected most of the newcomers were waiting for the upcoming concert. The placard on the bar said it was a local band, but not any that she recognized.

"What about him?" Sara asked while Elle dug through her wallet for cash to cover her portion of the tab.

"Hmm?"

"That guy at the end of the bar is totally checking you out," said Sara.

Elle glanced where Sara indicated and met the gaze of a man who smiled and raised his glass to her. She ignored the gesture and turned back to paying the bill. "He's cute, I guess."

"I bet he would give you his number if you asked."

"Good thing I'm not asking," Elle said as she stuffed her wallet back into her purse.

"C'mon, Elle. Why not?"

"Because I'm not interested."

"Well you should be. How long has it been?" Sara asked.

"I don't see how that's any of your business."

"Elle, this is me you're talking to. Of course it's my business."

Elle ignored her.

"You'd be singing a different tune if you were gettin' some," Sara muttered as she sucked up the last of her cocktail.

"Want to go back to my place and crack open a bottle of wine?" Elle asked as she got bumped yet again by someone trying to order a drink. "It will be much quieter. Not to mention cheaper."

"Might as well. Lenny works until nine tonight. Can I ride with you and then he can just pick me up after work?"

"Of course," said Elle. As she stood, Elle felt the two drinks go straight to her head, causing her to stumble right into the arms of a nearby stranger.

"I'm so—" She was about to apologize until she realized just whose arms had caught her.

"Well, well, well. Look who it is," said Raiden with his usual smirk. He helped her up and Elle had to grip the bar to keep from landing back in his arms. When did she become such a lightweight?

"What are you doing here?" she asked with more effort than it should have required to keep from slurring. God, how strong did they pour those drinks?

"I'm here for the show," he said slowly, and Elle could see worry in his face, which only irritated her. "Are you okay?" he asked.

"I'm fine," she said. But she wasn't fine. The room was starting to spin, and then everything went dark.

Three

The pale light filtering through Elle's bedroom window was too much for her throbbing head. As she lay there trying to summon the strength to move downstairs where the ibuprofen was, she wondered how she got home last night. But the more she thought about it, the more she realized she didn't remember anything about the evening. She climbed out of bed and grabbed a robe from the foot of the bed. Looking down at her pajamas, she figured she must not have been in too bad a shape if she managed to change out of her clothes…but then why couldn't she remember any of it?

In the kitchen, Elle downed the pills with a large glass of water and stared out the window over the kitchen sink, thinking that relief couldn't come fast enough. *What the hell happened last night?* She refilled the glass and was about to take another sip when there was a noise from the living room. It sounded like a grunt or a snore. She froze. Someone else was in her house.

With as little noise as possible, she grabbed the broom from the pantry and crept down the hall to the living room. There was Raiden Kane asleep on her couch. Not sure how she'd walked through the room without noticing him, she cautiously approached and tapped him gently with the broom handle.

"Hey," she said, but he just groaned and rolled over. "Hey," she said, much louder this time, and his eyes started to open.

"You're awake," he said, rubbing his face with both hands.

"Yes, I'm awake," she seethed. "What are you doing in my house?"

Raiden's face broke into a huge yawn before he answered. "You were drugged."

"What do you mean I was drugged?"

He sat up. "What's the last thing you remember?"

Elle mentally retraced her steps starting from when she left work. Sara met her at The Crocodile. They were about to leave when she ran into Raiden.

And then…and then everything was a blank. Elle lowered herself onto the solid wood coffee table across from him.

"I was roofied," she whispered, and Raiden gave a grave nod.

"But who? How?"

"We don't know. But the police notified the bar so they could be on the lookout for any other suspicious behavior. I think they might be going through surveillance video as well, but that place was pretty crowded."

"The police were involved?"

"We didn't know what had happened, so we called 911. The paramedics arrived and eventually told us the best thing for you was to sleep it off."

"Wait," she said, "so they let a drugged female leave with a male that wasn't her husband?"

"Sara was with me the whole time. I explained that I worked for your father and gave them all my contact info."

"Did you call my father?" asked Elle.

"I thought about it, but I decided not to when there wasn't much else to be done. Sara told me he had Logan for the weekend and I didn't want either of them to worry."

Elle nodded. "That was probably best."

"So Sara and I brought you home, she got you

changed and into bed, and then her boyfriend…Kenny?"

"Lenny," Elle corrected.

"Yeah, Lenny came and picked her up."

"Why did you stay?" she asked.

"I wanted to make sure you were all right. And I thought someone should be here when you woke up."

"Thank you," she said. "I don't know what else to say other than thank you."

"I'm just glad I ran into you when I did. Chances are whoever drugged you would have swept in if I hadn't been there."

Elle shuddered thinking about what almost happened. She remembered the guy at the bar, the one Sara had pointed it out. Could it have been him?

"Hey," he said, placing a steady hand on her knee. "You're safe."

"Because of you."

He shrugged it off. "Now that you're up, I should probably head home. Your couch is nice and all, but not exactly the most comfortable place to sleep."

"Sorry, it wasn't what I had in mind when I was shopping for it."

He laughed.

"Can I make you breakfast before you go?" she asked. "I mean, it's the least I can do after what you did for me last night."

There was the boyish smirk again. "Don't feel like you owe me anything. But that being said, I wouldn't want to say no to having breakfast with a beautiful woman."

Elle felt the color rushing to her cheeks. But then she frowned. "Can I ask you something? Something more personal?"

"Okay," he said.

"It's just that I'm so confused," she started. "I mean last night you went above and beyond to help me out when you could have left me with Sara or called my dad. And then I see how good you are with Logan, who adores you—he can't stop asking if we'll get to see you again."

The look on his face told Elle that he knew exactly where she was going with this, but he didn't stop her.

"And so I don't understand how you can be the same man who is leaving his wife and unborn child."

"That's because you're only half right," he said, looking her right in the eye. "Yes, Maureen is pregnant. But it's not my child she's carrying."

Elle sucked in a breath, and Raiden nodded. "Hence the divorce."

"Did you know she was having an affair?" She regretted the question as soon as she said it. It was far too personal.

He inhaled deeply and then let it all spill out. Elle realized he had been wanting to talk to someone about this for a while.

"Less than two years into the marriage, there was a marked difference in our relationship. I tried everything to fix it, even suggested counseling— which she agreed to—but in the end I knew she was just going through the motions. Maureen traveled a lot for her work and I thought a romantic gesture might help kick-start things, so I decided to surprise her and showed up at her hotel room in LA. Only—" The words got stuck in his throat. "Only she wasn't alone."

"Is that when you found out she was pregnant," Elle asked.

He shook his head. "Even with what I'd discovered, I still thought we could survive this. That if she just ended the affair, we could start again. A couple weeks later she found out she was pregnant and I filed for divorce that afternoon."

"I'm so sorry," said Elle as she placed a hand on his knee. She knew the words didn't quite cut it, but it was the only thing she could think to say.

"You still up for making breakfast?" Raiden finally asked. "Because I could just as easily head home. Don't feel like you have to."

"Nonsense," she said, standing up and wrapping the loosening robe tighter around herself.

"I'll just use the restroom real quick," he said, standing as well. "Try and freshen up somewhat."

"It's just down the hall," she said, and then caught the small grin on his face. "But you knew that already."

He nodded and headed for the bathroom.

The fridge was fully stocked from a recent grocery run, and Elle was able to round up eggs and bacon. She had just laid the bacon into a hot pan when Raiden walked into the kitchen.

"Do you mind if I throw my t-shirt into the dryer?" he asked, sniffing the collar of it. "Just in case."

She whisked the eggs while trying to remember if there was anything in it at the moment, but then remembered she had folded the last load yesterday before going into work.

"Yeah, it's empty. Go ahead," she said, pointing to the small room off the kitchen. "There's a steam fresh setting, should only take a few minutes."

"Thanks," he said and disappeared into the laundry room.

A minute later, Elle heard the machine beep and Raiden calling for help.

"It's saying to add water," he said.

"Hold on," she shouted, setting down the bowl. She filled a large measuring cup with water and walked into the other room, where she was halted by the sight of a shirtless Raiden. In addition to the well-defined muscles she had suspected were hiding beneath the fitted shirts, he was sporting even more beautifully designed inked artwork. In that moment she couldn't focus on what any of them were, she just knew that the whole effect was…amazing. 'Panty-dropping,' as her friend Sara would be apt to say. Elle had always cringed at the phrase, but if ever there was a good use for it….

"Is that the water?" asked Raiden.

"Huh?" She looked at the cup in her hand. "Oh, yeah."

The corner of his mouth went up and her cheeks burned, knowing that he was fully aware of the effect he was having on her. With a tight jaw, she moved in front of him, ignoring the heat radiating from his half-naked body, and opened the drawer to fill the reservoir. She turned back around and forced herself to look up into his eyes and not at his chest, which was rising and falling with his quickened breath, much like her own.

"It should work now," she said, barely louder than a whisper.

The cup was taken from her and she furrowed her

brow as he placed it on the dryer behind her. And then both of his hands were on either side of her face and he was kissing her.

She didn't realize she had raised her hands until she felt his warm chest pressed against her palms. A hand left her face and moved down to undo the knot on her robe before sliding in and underneath the tank top to her back. Her breath hitched as he pulled her body tight against his. She lifted her head to try and catch a breath as Raiden's mouth moved to her neck, causing what little air was left to leave her lungs. It was too much. She had spent the last two years keeping anyone that might hurt her at arm's length, and now, in her laundry room of all places, Raiden was showing her what she had been missing this whole time. She took a deep breath and grabbed his head, forcing his lips against hers. He responded eagerly and she could feel a low growl escape him.

His hands were at her shoulders, pushing the robe down, and she had to let go of him. He was just lifting the hem of her shirt when Elle caught a whiff of something.

"The bacon," she said, pulling away from him.

"Screw the bacon," he muttered as he turned with her and pressed her back against the wall. She wrapped a leg around his waist and Raiden's hand was quick to grasp it and the other thigh, lifting her off the floor. With her arms around his neck, Elle went back to filling his mouth with her tongue. But then the smoke detector started going off and even Raiden couldn't ignore that.

Disappointed, they rushed into the smoky kitchen but found no flames. She turned the burner off and put a nearby lid over the crispy bacon while Raiden opened the back door and started fanning the screeching smoke alarm. When it finally silenced, Raiden stopped waving his arms only to have it start right back up again. He went back to fanning it, and Elle broke out into laughter. And to think this all started with a kiss. The alarm went silent again and Raiden held his breath waiting to see if it would go off once more.

Elle stifled her giggles as he walked over and leaned against the counter, trapping her between his arms.

"Now where were we?" he asked with a smile.

She cleared her throat. "Bacon is off the menu," she said, trying to ignore the desire to kiss him. There would be no burning bacon to save her this time. "But I can still make the scrambled eggs."

He politely pushed off the counter, but Elle could still see the disappointment in his eyes and she felt a twinge of guilt. She wanted him—God, how she wanted him! But she wasn't sure if she was ready yet.

"I should probably head home," he said and went into the laundry room to grab his shirt.

"Are you sure?" she asked when he walked back out, holding his shirt along with her robe.

"I'm sure it's for the best," he said, handing her the robe before putting his shirt back on. "You had a rough night."

"Oh. Okay." She wrapped the robe around herself once again and followed him to the front door. "Thank you. Again. In case I haven't said it enough yet."

"Anytime," he said and leaned into her right side, where she thought he was going to kiss her cheek. But then he grabbed his car keys from the stand behind her, and once again she felt the irritation of expecting a kiss that never came.

"What about my car?" she asked.

"It's out there. Sarah drove your car home and I followed in mine. The keys are behind you."

She looked behind her to see them sitting on the bench.

"Take care," he said, opening the door.

"Until next time."

The corner of his mouth curled up. "Until next time."

It was only five o'clock in the afternoon, but Elle was already enjoying the therapeutic benefits of a hot bath and a chilled glass of chardonnay. She took a sip and glanced at the cell phone she always kept within reach when Logan wasn't by her side. But it wasn't Logan who filled her thoughts at the moment.

Elle set the half-empty glass on the ledge of her jetted tub and dried her fingers before picking up the phone and dialing it.

Cassie quickly picked up on the other end.

"Hey, Elle, what's going on?" she answered in her typical bubbly voice.

"Hi, Cassie. I'm so sorry to bother you on a Saturday, but I have a favor to ask."

"Sure, what is it?" she asked.

"Raiden Kane was helping me with something," Elle said, not really lying. "And now I have a question for him, but it turns out I don't have his number. Any chance you have it?"

"Sure, let me go look it up," said Cassie. "You know, your dad should have it as well. Probably memorized even."

"I know, but he has Logan for the weekend and I'm afraid if I call, Logan will want to interrupt whatever fun activity they're in the middle of to talk to me. For hours." Okay, now Elle was completely lying.

"Gotcha. Here it is, are you ready?"

Elle looked around the bathroom and realized she had nothing to write with. "Actually, could you just text me?"

"Of course. Hey, Elle?"

"Yes?"

"You're not the first girl to call me for Raiden's cell number."

"Don't be silly." Elle forced a nervous laugh. "It's not like that."

"Sure. Well, talk to you later."

"Wait."

"Yeah?"

"Do you usually give it out?" Elle asked.

"Nope," said Cassie. "I figure if they don't already have it, they must not need it."

"Then why'd you give it to me?"

"Because I can tell he likes you. Talk to you later, Elle."

"You too, Cassie. Thanks."

Elle set down her phone and picked the wine glass up again. The text came through just as she took another sip. The text with Raiden's phone number. But now what was she going to do with it?

She closed her eyes and remembered the kiss in her laundry room only hours before and a shiver swept through her. How long had it been since a man had touched her like that? Until this morning, she hadn't even realized how much she had missed it.

Elle drained the rest of her wine and picked the phone back up. She called the number Cassie had sent before her courage vanished.

After the first ring, she wondered if he was busy. And then with the second ring she began to realize what a mistake this was. Halfway through the third she began praying it would go to voicemail.

"Raiden Kane," he announced before the fourth ring.

"Raiden, hi, this is Elle," she said, realizing her voice sounded way too breathy due to the hot bath and nerves.

"Elle." She could hear the smile in his voice. "To what do I owe the pleasure?"

"I was wondering…" Oh God, what was she wondering? Why had she called him? She sat up straighter in the tub, causing water to splash against the sides.

"Are you in—" he started, "Are you in a bathtub?"

Shit. "I—yes. Um, the reason I was calling—"

"Is everything okay?" he asked. "You aren't feeling any more after-effects, are you?"

"Yes, I'm fine. I just called to see if you would like to have dinner with me. At a restaurant," she hastily added in case he thought dinner was code for something else.

"Are you asking me on a date?"

"I suppose," she said slowly. "Are you interested?"

"How did you get my number?" he asked. "Did your father give it to you?"

"I called Cassie," she said quietly.

"And she gave it to you, just like that?"

"I may have led her to believe it was work-related."

"I see," he said. "Well, I would love to have dinner with you. Did you have somewhere special in mind?"

"Um…." She hadn't thought this far ahead, hadn't thought she would actually work up the nerve to call him. She racked her brain, thinking of her favorite Seattle restaurants. "How about Capital Grille? Do you know where it is?"

He chuckled. "I'm familiar with it. What time? Now?"

Elle looked down at her naked body. "How about in an hour?"

"That's right," he said slowly. "You're in the bathtub."

She was grateful he couldn't see her blushing.

"See you in an hour, Raiden."

"Looking forward to it."

The Uber driver dropped Elle off in front of the restaurant with ten minutes to spare. It had taken a whole glass of wine just to summon the courage to call Raiden, and she feared how much it would take to relax around him. Plus she didn't care for Saturday night downtown drivers under the best of conditions. Throw nerves and alcohol into the mix and it was a recipe for disaster.

The rich woods and soft lighting of The Capital Grille made it warm and inviting, but they did nothing to calm Elle's butterflies as she walked through the front door. How many years had it been since she'd been on a date, let alone a first date? She tried telling herself that she had already kissed the man, the hard part was over, but if anything, it just made things worse. Maybe she should call and tell him something came up.

"How many tonight?" the hostess at the front booth asked, interrupting her indecisiveness.

"Um," she said, nervously smoothing out the front of her skirt. She was still contemplating leaving—surely it wasn't too late—when she felt a hand on the small of her back, giving her a start.

"We'll be sitting at the bar this evening," Raiden's voice said from behind her.

She turned to see him dressed similarly to the first time she met him at her father's home—casual button-down shirt with the sleeves rolled up, and right then she decided that was her favorite look on him.

"Right that way," said the hostess. "Enjoy your evening."

Raiden guided her to two empty seats at the mahogany bar.

"Perfect timing," she said, slipping off her sweater and hanging it on the red-leather trimmed high back bar stool.

"Almost. I live in the apartments above and saw you arrive."

"Oh," she said. "I had no idea."

"I figured as much," he said with a shrug. "It was a great choice, though, so who was I to complain."

"Good evening, Mr. Kane," the bartender said as he placed two cocktail napkins on the bar. "What can I get you this evening?"

Raiden gave her a sheepish grin as he answered. "I will have the usual, and my companion here would like…."

"A glass of chardonnay," she finished for him. The bartender nodded and walked away. "Come in here now and then, I see," she said.

"They have a decent happy hour and it's

convenient," he said. "Better than having a drink after work and then having to make that drive home."

"True," she nodded. "Probably safer as well."

"Exactly."

"But does anyone from the firm meet up with you here?"

"On occasion," he said with a tilt of his head.

"So what you're saying is that you usually drink alone?"

"I've got Del here to keep me company," he said with a smile as the bartender set down Elle's wine and a tumbler of amber liquid on the rocks for Raiden.

She looked at the compass tattoo on his forearm and remembered what her father said about Raiden not being the only person in the legal field having tattoos. And while admittedly she had never seen the naked chest of any of Raiden's co-workers, she still doubted they had any to the extent of his own artwork.

"Do you get along with your co-workers?" she asked.

"Sure. I mean they seem to like me."

"But you're different," she said without explanation.

"Is that a good thing?" he asked with a smile as

he took a sip from his glass and their eyes stayed locked, even as he set the glass back down.

"I'll have to let you know," she whispered.

"Will you two need menus?" Del the bartender asked, and Elle was finally able to pull her gaze away from Raiden.

"Yes, please," said Raiden.

"So where are you from?" Elle asked after Del had walked away with their dinner orders.

"Ah, are we at this part of the date now? The twenty questions?"

"Are you saying I shouldn't be trying to get to know you better?"

"No, not at all," he said with a broad grin. "Okay then. I'm originally from California, but I moved to Oregon my senior year of high school, then came up here for law school."

"What about—"

"Wait. It's your turn to answer the question."

"Easy," she said, sitting up straight in the bar stool. "Seattle. Born and raised. Well, in the area at least. When Jeannie and my dad got married we moved into the house in Woodinville."

"So Jeannie's your step-mom?"

"Sorry, it's my turn to ask again."

He groaned but gestured for her to continue. Elle

was enjoying this game.

"Where're your parents?"

"My mom currently lives in Portland and my father died when I was fourteen. She never remarried."

Elle's face fell. "Oh. I'm so sorry."

"Don't worry about it," he said, taking a sip. "It was a heart attack. Nothing anyone could've done about it."

Elle placed a hand on his knee. "We don't have to play this game anymore if you don't want."

He turned to her with a smile. "Really? One uncomfortable answer and you're ready to throw in the towel?"

"You're right," she said, shaking her head. "Of course not. Let's see, I guess it's my turn to tell you about my parents."

"And then I think I should get a turn choosing the question."

"Fair enough," she said.

By the time their food arrived, Elle no longer felt the nervousness she had experienced walking in the front door. She never imagined Raiden would be this comfortable to talk to. And as she became more at ease with him, Elle found herself touching him more, a playful shove when he teased her, a hand against his shoulder as she laughed at something he said. She wanted to blame it on the wine, but the truth was she had barely touched her glass. Elle knew she was in trouble.

Three hours later and the bar was reaching capacity. But the last thing Raiden wanted was to say good night to Elle. Every time she threw her head back in laughter, he wanted to kiss her beautiful neck, and more. It was tempting to invite her up to his apartment, where they could continue their evening in a less crowded environment. After her hesitation in the kitchen that morning, though, he was worried the suggestion would spook her. At least he had a good excuse for leaning in close to her every time he had something to say to her. And when he did, he would catch a whiff of her intoxicating perfume again. Did she have any idea the effect that stuff had on him whenever he was this close to her?

But then Del had to go and lay down the bill. He and Elle had both moved on to only water, so it made sense.

He reached for it, but she beat him to it.

"My treat," she said as she pulled out her credit card. "I'm the one who asked you out."

"But you came all this way when all I had to do was walk down the stairs."

"It's not far for me. And besides, I owe you for saving me last night."

He leaned in even closer. "I'm the one that's grateful I was there. No repayment needed."

"Oh, well," she said as Del took the check and her card.

"Fine. But then you have to let me pay for the second date."

"You're assuming there will be a second date," she said with a wicked smile.

"I'm liking my odds so far," he said and watched the color rush to her cheeks.

It was obvious that Elle felt the same attraction to him that he felt for her, no matter how much she tried to deny it.

Del handed the card and slip back to her.

"It's probably time for me to get home," she said as she signed it.

"I'll walk you out to wait for a cab,' he said with a sigh.

Together they winded their way through the people waiting for a seat out to the valet station, where he asked someone to hail a taxi.

"I had a really great time tonight, Elle," he said, turning back to her and brushing the hair from her face.

"Are you waiting for me to ask you on a second

date?" she asked with a smile.

He laughed. "If you don't, I will." An empty taxi pulled up to the curb. "Because I would really like to see you again. In fact, the sooner, the better."

She responded by getting up on her toes and kissing him. He could still taste the cherry from the dessert they had shared. Her chest pressed against his, and it was all he could do not to drag her upstairs to his bedroom that instant.

There was a cough and Raiden knew if Elle didn't get in the cab soon, it would be leaving without her. Not that that was a bad thing.

She stepped back. "I should go," she said. But Raiden could see the struggle in her eyes again. "I'll call you." She climbed into the taxi and he shut the door, giving her a wave as the vehicle pulled away.

He walked into his apartment to hear the intercom buzzing.

"Hello?" he asked, confused.

He thought he must be imagining Elle's voice coming through the speaker.

"Buzz me in before I change my mind."

Four

When the elevator door opened, Elle found
Raiden waiting for her on the other side of it.

"I saw the cab drive off with you in it," he said.

"I made him circle back around," she said
quietly, still pressed against the back of the metal
box. "I realized I wasn't ready to say goodnight. Not
yet."

The door started to close and Raiden put a hand
against it, forcing it to slide back into the wall.

"Would you like to come with me?" he asked,
holding out the other hand.

It wasn't too late, she realized. She could shake
her head no and push the button for the lobby. He
might never speak to her again, but he would let her

go.

"Yes," she said, taking it, and he pulled her out of the elevator, letting the doors close behind her.

Her legs felt unsteady as they walked two doors down to his apartment. As much as she wanted this, a small voice in her head reminded how horribly wrong this could go. But as they walked in the door, Raiden pulled her into him and she told the voice to shut up. She stumbled backwards from the weight of his kiss and met the wall with her back. Her fingers fumbled with the buttons of his shirt and he saved her the effort by pulling it up over his head before helping her out of her camisole. He made quick work of the strapless bra beneath it before cupping a hand around her left breast and his lips around the other. She ran a hand roughly through his hair and he sucked even harder on her nipple.

"Oh God," she panted.

He stood up and kissed her neck, then her ear, before coming back to her mouth. He tasted so good. One of his hands slid down over her ass and up under the skirt. His thumb traced the edge of her lacy underwear to the front, where he slipped underneath, and she moaned as she reached for his jeans and began working desperately to undo them. It was hard to focus with his thumb gently stroking her. It was almost too much for her poor deprived body. When she finally succeeded in pushing his pants and underwear down enough, he kicked off his shoes and shimmied out of them. Raiden, standing stark naked in his front hall, knelt before her and gently slid the lace down her now quivering legs. She stepped out of them and when she lifted the second leg, he took hold of it, putting it over his left shoulder. He pushed her skirt up and kissed the inside of her thigh. Her body slid down the wall just a quarter of an inch, and it was all he needed to make contact.

"Please," she moaned, and he looked up at her.

"Do you want me to stop?" he asked.

She shook her head and tried to say no, but no sound came out. Raiden grinned and started working her with his tongue. But it wasn't long before the one leg she was standing began to give way and she slid even further down the wall. Seconds later he released her leg and stood to face her.

"Not sure I could I support you much longer from that angle," he said with a huge grin.

"Sorry," she mumbled.

"Don't apologize," he said, pressing his mouth against her ear. "I love that I make you so weak in the knees." And before she could respond, he hooked both arms beneath her thighs, lifting her off the floor, putting them in the same position as they had been in earlier that day in her laundry room. But this time, the only thing between them was the skirt, currently hiked up around her waist, and as he slowly slid into her, she groaned. Why had she been so resistant to this? He gave her a second and she relished the feeling of him inside her, but then he withdrew and quickly thrust into her again, and this time, she gave a little scream.

"Harder," she breathed into his ear.

He did as she demanded and she dug her nails into his back as he continued to drive into her, again and again, her shoulder blades slamming against the wall each time.

And then she could feel the heat in her chest rising up her neck, across her face. She was close—God, she was so close.

"Faster," she begged and again he answered her pleas, quickening his pace, and something inside her exploded. She clenched her thighs around his hips and pulled at his hair. Her whole body was at his mercy as she succumbed to the pleasure, letting the last powerful wave roll though her.

With one last thrust, Raiden groaned as she felt his body tighten against hers. She was still trying to catch her breath when his arms gave out and her legs fell to the floor with a thud.

He leaned against her and she knew he was the only reason she wasn't sliding down the wall into a puddle on the floor right now.

"Wow," she said breathlessly. "That was definitely a first for me, being fucked against the wall."

He grinned at her profanity. "Oh, we're just getting started."

Elle woke the next morning feeling a little sore, but blissfully satisfied. It wasn't until the third round that they had finally moved into the bedroom, where she had crashed shortly after with Raiden at her side. His hand was on her sternum now and she placed one of her own over it, causing him to moan. He shifted closer to her.

"Mmm, you smell good," he said groggily into her ear.

"After last night, I can't imagine I smell like anything other than sweat."

"Exactly. Sweat and sex," he said, making her laugh. "I smell sex and candy here." He crooned the old '90s song as he rubbed his scratchy chin against her neck and she broke into full-on giggles.

"Stop," she begged through the laughter.

Raiden stopped and pushed up on an arm to look down at her. She stared into his light blue eyes while he brushed her hair back with a free hand. Elle could only imagine what a tangled mess it was, but she didn't care. She loved the way he was looking at her right now. Her heart swelled and she ignored the little voice in the back of her mind saying that this was going to hurt like hell the further she went. But maybe not, said a stronger, more confident voice within her.

"What are you thinking?" he asked, and she saw a trace of worry in his face.

"Nothing," she said with a smile. "Just how glad I am that I made the cabbie turn back around."

He kissed her nose. And then her neck. His stubble prickled her skin as he left kisses down her torso, but this time she didn't mind. He repositioned himself between her legs but kept his mouth at her waist, kissing her hip bones and flicking his tongue across her belly.

"What should we do for breakfast?" he asked between kisses.

"God," she moaned, "I can't even think about breakfast right now."

"You're right," he teased. "It's too late for breakfast. What should we do for lunch?"

Elle glanced at the clock by his bed and shot up, nearly sending a knee into Raiden's chin.

"Crap," she said, "I have to go!"

"Go? But I thought—"

"I have to pick up Logan," she told him, jumping

out of bed. "Where are my clothes?"

"Kitchen, I believe." He climbed out as well and helped her find the scattered pieces.

"I have to get home and shower before I head over," she said, slipping her foot into a shoe. "I can't show up looking like this." She looked in a framed mirror by the door. With bed-head and the slightly smudged left-over mascara, she had a boudoir look about her. Better than she had feared, but not how she wanted to pick up her son.

"Do you think it would be easier to use Uber from here, or just go down and grab a cab?" she asked, checking the phone in her purse for messages. None from her dad, thank God. Sara had checked in though. And she had been right, Elle had *so* much to tell her now.

"I'll drive you home," said Raiden, pulling on jeans.

"You don't have to do that," she said, looking back up at him—still shirtless—and sucking in a breath. His own hair was equally disheveled and it was sexy as hell. What she wouldn't give to just spend the whole day here. In his bed.

He took one of her hands and kissed the palm. "I want to if it means getting to spend fifteen more minutes with you."

When they arrived at Elle's house, Raiden leaned

across to kiss her goodbye. And as she reluctantly pulled away from him and saw the look in his beautiful blue eyes, she knew in that moment that last night was not going to be a one-time thing.

"Call me," he said and waited until she was inside before pulling away.

Elle got a pot of coffee going before running up to take a quick shower. She barely remembered the drive to Woodinville as she relived the night before. Her brain only changed tracks when she arrived at her father's house.

Elle was in the kitchen with Jeannie, helping with the finishing touches for dinner when the doorbell rang.

"Will you get that for me?" her father asked as he slid in and took over the salad she was tossing.

"Um, all right." Why couldn't her father answer his own front door?

She had her answer the second she opened it. There was Raiden, looking just as surprised to see her.

"Hello," he said. "I wasn't expecting you to be here."

"My father invited you, didn't he?" she asked.

"He needed me to bring over some documents for him to sign."

"That's the excuse he used to get you here?"

"I suppose he thought you would be gone by now."

"Logan and I always stay for dinner," she said and Raiden laughed. "Come in." They walked out to the back patio, where Marcus and Jeannie were setting food out on the table.

"Look who I found on your front porch, Dad."

"Oh, Raiden," he said, pretending to look surprised. "I forgot I asked you to stop by."

"You know Dad," said Elle, "as a lawyer, I would expect you to be a better liar."

Raiden and Marcus both looked wounded. "That's a low blow," said Raiden.

Elle, still in a playful mood from her weekend with him, stuck her tongue out at them.

"Since you're here," her father said to Raiden, "you might as well join us for dinner. I'm sure there's more than enough food."

"And look," said Elle, "there even happens to be a place setting for you already. Right here next to mine. Imagine that."

There was a twinkle in her father's eye as he gave her a smile. Marcus wasn't fooling anyone.

After dinner, Elle cornered her father in the kitchen.

"I know what you were trying to do tonight, but

it wasn't necessary."

"Why would you say that?" he asked as he loaded plates into the dishwasher. "You two seemed to get along quite well at dinner."

"That's because we went out last night."

"You did?" he asked, standing with a stunned look on his face. "How did this happen?"

"I decided to take your advice and call him," she said. "We had dinner. Last night." Elle decided not to bring up what happened Friday night just yet. She was in too good a mood right now.

"And did he tell you about Maureen?" he said, wiping his hands on a dish towel and leaning against the counter with his arms folded across his chest.

"He did."

"And did you share your own story?"

Elle looked down at her hands. "Let's not go there right now."

The familiar sigh escaped him. "You have to deal with it sometime, Sweetie."

"I know, Dad, but not now. Please? It's been such a good weekend."

He placed his hands on her shoulders and gave a smile.

"I'm sorry I brought it up. I just want you to be happy. But I'm glad to see you getting out there again. Raiden is a great guy."

She nodded and smiled. "I know, Dad, I know."

The clock was reading half past nine and everyone was back around the now-empty dining table, including Logan, who had crawled into Elle's lap twenty minutes ago and fallen asleep shortly after. Raiden looked over at her to see that she was still gently rocking side to side. He wondered if she even knew she was still doing it.

Spending the evening with his boss was not how he imagined the perfect end to a weekend, but sitting here next to Elle was exactly where he wanted to be.

Marcus yawned, and Raiden knew all good things must come to an end.

"I think it's past all of our bedtimes," said Elle. She tried to get up still holding Logan, but Raiden jumped from his seat to carefully take him from her arms.

"You really wore him out," she said with a smile as she relinquished the boy.

The three of them moved to the front door, accompanied by Marcus and Jeannie.

"Thanks for dinner, sir," Raiden said, and Marcus gave him a friendly pat on the back as he held the door open for them.

"Of course," Marcus said with a twinkle in his eye. "It was our pleasure."

Elle rolled her eyes. "Good night, Dad. Thank you as always." She kissed his cheek and hugged her stepmother.

"Drive carefully, you two," Jeannie said.

"I'll see you in the office tomorrow, Raiden," Marcus called out, and Raiden gave him a nod just before the door shut.

"I can't believe he's still asleep," Raiden said as placed Logan in the car seat and let Elle strap him in.

"He's a pretty heavy sleeper," she said as she closed the rear passenger car door. "It's hard to wake him once he's out." She gave his shirt a tug and he leaned down to kiss her softly on the lips. "Thank you for the wonderful weekend," she whispered.

"I hope it won't be the last," he said.

"Could I entice you to come over for dinner this week?" she asked.

"I don't know," he teased. "You did burn the bacon last time you tried to cook for me."

"That wasn't entirely my fault," she said, laughing.

"True. Dinner would be nice. How does Tuesday work?"

"Tuesday would be good," she said. "We eat at six."

"Then I will see you at six on Tuesday," he said, kissing her one last time.

"Can't wait," she said with a little smile as she slipped into her car and drove away.

A little before six, Raiden showed up on Elle's front porch with a bottle of wine and a bouquet of pink calla lilies.

"These are beautiful," she said, taking them into the kitchen.

"And I have something for you as well," he said to Logan, who was thrilled to have Raiden in his house. "I saw your game system and wondered if you have this game yet?" Raiden gave Logan the newest kart racing game.

"I don't know," said Logan. "Do we have this one, Mommy?"

Elle looked from Logan, who was excited about something new, to Raiden, who was confused.

"He's never played on it before," she said quietly.

"Oh, then I guess maybe the new game is for your Mom."

"She never plays it either," said Logan.

Elle saw the light go off in Raiden's head and she quickly turned to the sink to get some fresh water for the flowers. She had debated for months about just tossing the stupid thing.

"Will you teach me how to play it?" Logan asked

Raiden.

"Only if your mom says it's okay."

She turned back around with a smile. "It's fine. It's about time we got some use out of it."

"Yay!" Logan started dragging Raiden back towards the living room.

"Just hit play game on the remote and everything will set up for you," she called out to them. "Dinner will be done in fifteen!"

Logan had requested spaghetti for their special guest, and now that the noodles were cooking and the bread was in the oven, all that was left was for the timer to go off. Elle moved into the living room and sat on the arm of the sofa to watch the boys play their video game. It was entertaining since neither was any good, and they both broke into laughter when one of them ran into a wall or got blown up. Logan kept getting turned around and Raiden would put his controller down to help Logan get going in the right direction.

Elle remembered the few times she would try to play with Jason and how competitive he got, even when she didn't know how to play. It was never any fun.

She shook her head. Jason did not deserve to be intruding on this moment.

The timer went off.

"All right, you guys. Time for dinner."

Raiden sat on the couch, flipping through an entertainment magazine while waiting for Elle. Twenty minutes later she came down the stairs looking exhausted but happy. He couldn't help but notice that she was glowing more these past few days. He wondered if he had anything to do with that.

"Sorry," she said, sitting on the coffee table in front of him just as she had done that Saturday morning. "Some nights it takes longer than others."

"I don't mind," he said, brushing her hair from her face. "I don't have to stay either. You look like you've had a long day."

"Do I look that bad?" she asked with a laugh.

"No. You look beautiful," he said. "Tired, but beautiful."

Her response was physical as she climbed onto his lap and took his face in both her hands before giving him a long, deep kiss. Raiden pulled her blouse from her pants and slid his palms up her back. She sat up and started unbuttoning the blouse until he took over for her, but she simply went to work on his own shirt buttons. She was more nimble and succeeded in opening his shirt first. He could feel her finger tracing along his chest as he struggled with the last one. Why did women's buttons have to be so much tinier?

"The artwork is so beautiful," she said.

"Which one?" he asked, exposing one of her shoulders.

"All of them." Her finger moved to the faded scar tissue just below his right shoulder.

"What is this from?" she asked.

"Another tattoo. My first one," he said, grazing his lips across her naked shoulder. "I had it removed several years ago."

"Why?" She had a small frown on her face, and Raiden kissed the corner of it.

"Because it was ugly. It was my first one and I didn't know what I was doing."

"I wish I had seen it. Maybe it wasn't as ugly as you thought."

Raiden kissed her, thankful that she had never laid eyes upon it. Thankful that part of his life was behind him. And here in front of him was a beautiful, smart woman that wanted him to be a part of her life.

"If I were to carry you to your bedroom right now," he said, and Elle gave a sly smile at his words, "would we wake Logan? Or should I just make love to you right here on this couch?"

She leaned in close to his ear. "You can take me

wherever you want," she whispered. "That kid could sleep through an earthquake."

Raiden stood, keeping her legs wrapped around him. "Then let's go make an earthquake," he said, carrying her up the stairs as she giggled.

The tangled sheet barely covered their naked bodies as they lie recovering in her bed.

"Are you sure Logan slept through all that?" Raiden asked, propped on his side facing Elle. "I'd hate to be responsible for traumatizing the poor kid."

She nodded. "Once he falls asleep, that kid is dead to the world. Sometimes after he falls asleep, I'll mess with him, make him do funny faces, and he just sleeps right through it." She started giggling, and Raiden laughed with her.

"I don't know that I could sleep through someone messing with my face," he said.

"I'm such a bad parent," she said, still laughing.

"No, you're not," he said, no longer laughing. "In fact, I think you're an awesome mom. You're doing such an incredible job raising him all on your own."

Her expression was a mix of pride and humility. "Thank you," she said. "It's been hard, but it's nice to hear someone say that. Besides my dad, of course."

A question had been burning in Raiden's mind

all evening, and he finally saw his opportunity to ask it.

"Where *is* Logan's father?" But as soon as he voiced it and saw the look on her face, he worried what wound he had just risked opening.

When she didn't respond, he spoke again. "I mean, obviously you were married, right?

"Yes," she finally said, rolling onto her back. It was harder to see her face now in what little light was coming through the closed door. "His name was Jason."

She paused, and Raiden waited patiently.

"We were together for a long time. Then after Logan was born, things were different between us. It's hard to be a carefree couple when you have a baby. But I thought we were managing, that we were coping as best we could. We had a nanny for Logan at first. Then, at eighteen months, we thought it would be good for him to go to daycare and be around other children. He got sick a lot at first, just like any child being exposed to a bunch of new germs, but it was never anything serious," she said, giving a shrug. "But it made for many sleepless nights and a very cranky family." There was another long pause, and Raiden leaned in closer and could see the far-off look in her eye. She was reliving it. "It was Jason's turn to drop him off and I had already left for work. As they were about to head out the door, Logan puked all over Jason, which meant he couldn't go to daycare, and that Jason had to call in sick. He called me and we argued. He wanted me to come home and take care of Logan and I told him he needed to suck it up." She sighed. "By the time I got home that evening, Jason had packed his bags. He handed me a screaming baby and said this wasn't what he had signed up for. I guess he forgot the lines in our vows about in sickness and in health," she said with a forced laugh. "For better or for worse."

"How long ago was that?" asked Raiden.

"Two years ago," she said, rolling over to face him again, and Raiden scooted closer until their bodies were touching. "For the longest time I waited for him to come home, kept listening for the key in the lock. I'd swear sometimes that I had heard it. I was sure that after cooling down, he would come back to us. But when Logan's third birthday rolled around and he sent a birthday card postmarked from his parents' home back east, that was the moment my heart shattered."

"Who filed first?" Raiden asked, remembering how Maureen's pregnancy had forced him into quick action.

"Filed what?"

"For divorce," said Raiden.

Elle hesitated, and he could feel her whole body stiffen against his.

"Technically we're still married."

The alarms bells sounded loud and clear in Raiden's head. "What do you mean by technically?" he asked.

"Obviously we aren't together anymore, but neither of us has filed for a dissolution."

He pulled away from her and sat up straight. "But why not? After a two year absence, don't you think it's clear the marriage is over?"

"Yes," she said slowly. "But if he hasn't filed either…."

Raiden couldn't believe what he was hearing. "But what? Are you still hoping he'll come back? Am I just helping you to pass the time?"

"No, it's not like that," she said, sitting up next to him. "The whole thing is complicated, especially with a child involved. I wouldn't expect you to understand."

Raiden climbed out of bed and put his pants back on. "After all the shit you gave me about Maureen," he said, shaking his head. "I can't believe you're still married."

"So are you," she said.

"Not for lack of trying. And it won't even be an issue because she finally signed the dotted line this morning. You, however," he said, pointing a finger at her, "you can't even make an effort. Just in case." He slid his shirt on but didn't bother buttoning it up as he exited the bedroom. He marched downstairs to find his phone and car keys and could hear her coming towards him.

"Please, Raiden, where are you going?" she asked as he grabbed his stuff from the coffee table.

"Home, Elle," he said, looking at her wrapped in a sheet standing on the middle step. "I'm going home. After Maureen, I'm not willing to spend another second with someone, waiting to be their priority."

He walked out, slamming the door behind him.

Five

It had been an hour since Raiden had walked out the front door and Elle was still sitting on the couch, rehashing the entire argument. At first she wondered how he could be such a jerk. But as the minutes passed by, she came to realize that he had a point. How did she expect him to react?

Wrapping a blanket around herself, she got up and went to the extra bedroom upstairs and sat down at the desk. She opened a bottom drawer and pulled out the folder her father had given her shortly after Jason walked out. He knew long before she'd ever wanted to admit it. She had told him that she needed time to think about it and had shoved it away. Tonight was the first night she had laid eyes on it since then. Across the hall was the door to Logan's bedroom and she looked at it, knowing that if it was only her, she would have thrown in the towel a long time ago. Raiden's words ran through her mind again. Jason wasn't here, divorce or no divorce. So why was she putting her own life on hold waiting for someone who did not want to be a part of this family?

Marcus was on the phone when Elle approached the door to his office early the next morning, but he waved her in and she waited patiently.

"Elle, dear," he said when he finally ended the call. "Is everything all right?"

"Yes. I just wanted to give you this," she handed him a folder, "before I went into work."

"You really went out of your way. This must be important if you couldn't wait."

She nodded. "Those are the divorce papers."

Marcus froze, but then he smiled. "You're finally ready."

"Yes," was all she could say.

He opened the folder and flipped through the pages. "I may have to update a few things. I'll fax over anything that needs to be initialed or signed."

"Thank you," she said.

"The request for child support is missing, but I

can print out a new one."

"I'm not asking for child support."

"Are you sure?" asked Marcus.

"I want to make this as simple as possible, and I don't need anything from him."

He paused to study her and she was sure he was going to argue, but then he nodded. "Understood." His phone rang and he apologized for having to take it, leaving Elle to show herself out. She paused at Cassie's desk.

"Where is Raiden's office?" Elle asked her.

"It's down that hall, second door on the left," said Cassie.

"Thank you."

"I doubt he's in though."

Elle smiled and decided to check anyway, but it was empty, just as Cassie had predicted, so she made her way back to the reception area and waited for the elevator. When the doors opened, Raiden was among the group showing up to work. He said nothing as he walked by her and she summoned the courage to follow him to his office. He walked in, set his bag on the chair, and finally turned to face her.

"I think I made myself abundantly clear last night," he said.

"I know," she said. "And you were right. And I realize that it doesn't change anything, but I finally gave the paperwork to my father for him to file. I wanted you to know…" she took a breath, "I want to know that you were the first person that made moving on with my life seem worthwhile."

Raiden just stood there, looking at her. There were no expressions to read, no body language to decipher.

"That's all I wanted to say. And to say thank you." Still he said nothing, so she left. She kept her composure the whole walk to the elevator, and during the entire ride down to the lobby, out the door, and to her car parked on the street. But before she could start the car, she broke into tears. She finally grasped the fact that she had just lost something amazing because she'd been too afraid to let go.

Elle was late getting into work that day and she didn't really care.

By Friday afternoon, Elle was emotionally exhausted. She felt both a weight off her shoulder from filing for the divorce and making the decision to move on, as well as a hole in her heart, wishing Raiden could have been a part of that new life.

Deciding to call it a day, she called the nanny to say that she would be picking up Logan from preschool and headed out early. After treating him to dinner at his favorite fast food restaurant—a rare treat—they pulled up to the house, where Raiden was camped out on their front step.

"Hi," she said, approaching him with caution. She wanted to believe that he was giving her another chance, but a voice in the back of her mind warned her that this could be a final farewell.

He stood and took an equally hesitant step toward her. "Hey."

"Is Raiden here for dinner?" Logan asked, and they both looked at him. "Because we already ate."

Raiden laughed. "No worries. I just came to talk to your mom, if that's alright."

Logan looked from Raiden to Elle. "Okay," he said with a shrug and walked past the two of them to the locked front door.

"Do you want to come inside?" Elle asked, and Raiden nodded. She unlocked the door and they all stepped inside. "Logan, sweetie, why don't you go up and get your pajamas on?"

He nodded and made the trek upstairs.

"He always gets distracted," she said, setting her purse on the bench. "He'll be up there a while. Can I get you some water or anything?"

"I'm sorry," he said, and she started to feel a ray of hope.

But then the voice gave another warning. *He's*

sorry that he can't see you anymore.

"Oh," she said.

"I'm sorry that I got so mad when you told me you were still married."

"You had every right after everything you went through with your ex."

He nodded. "At first I couldn't understand why you wouldn't have cut all ties with him. But it's not just you, it's Logan's family as well. And I also remember that even after I found out about Maureen's affair, I still wanted it to work. I was still holding onto hope. It took her getting pregnant with his baby for me to realize that there was never going to be an us again."

Elle moved closer to him and placed her hands on his chest. But he continued before she could find any words.

"I don't want you to get divorced because of me," he said, placing his hands over hers. "I don't want you to make this decision for me only to be disappointed if I'm not the man you need."

She shook her head. "I'm not doing this for you. I did it for Logan and me."

"Are you sure?" he asked.

"Yes. This is something I should have done the day I knew Jason had no intention of coming back."

"What about Logan?"

"Logan deserves a mother who is happy. Who isn't sitting around waiting to see if his father will ever come back. If I'm happy with you, or someone else, or with just Logan and me, that's better than what we have." She paused, studying his bright blue eyes, the full lips that she knew would feel soft against her own. "But what about you?" she asked.

"What about me?" he asked with a frown.

"Would you be willing to give me a second chance?"

He smiled. "Why do you think I'm here?"

Raiden spent Friday night at their house. Then the next day, the three of them stopped at Raiden's apartment so he could change before taking Logan down to the waterfront, where they rode the giant ferris wheel. When Elle woke on Sunday morning with Raiden yet again at her side, she found herself wondering if it had been smart, from a mother's point of view, to allow a man she was only dating to spend the entire weekend with her and her son. Not to mention in her bed. But when she rolled over to face Raiden, who was still sleeping, she didn't care how selfish she was being because this felt good. Really good.

And it wasn't as if Logan had suffered from Raiden's presence. Most of the weekend had been spent entertaining him. In addition to The Great Wheel, they had visited the Pacific Science Center, and Raiden had mentioned visiting the zoo today. It was amazing how well Logan and Raiden got along.

As Elle studied Raiden lying before her, she knew he was going to be an awesome dad someday. For a brief moment, she wished she had chosen him instead of Jason. But then she wouldn't have ended up with Logan. Jason may have left her with a lot of heartache, but he gave her Logan, and she would be forever grateful for that. And now here was Raiden, helping the two of them put all the pieces back together without them even asking.

Raiden stirred, and then his eyes slowly opened.

"Morning," he rasped out when he caught her gaze.

"Sorry," she said, "was I thinking too hard?"

He smiled. "I don't think so. What were you thinking about?"

"Just how much fun I've had this weekend."

His grin stretched even wider. "Me too. I'd never been to any of the places we visited yesterday."

"Really?"

"Never had an opportunity to."

She kissed his lips. "Glad we could help."

Raiden brushed a hand along her cheek and slid a leg over hers, but before either could do anything else, little feet could be heard coming down the hall and they both froze. Elle suspected that Raiden felt the same as her and wasn't ready for Logan to see them in bed together like this. Fortunately the footsteps continued into the bathroom, but Elle knew this would be the next stop.

"Until next time," Raiden said before sliding out of bed and throwing on a t-shirt to go with the sweatpants he was already wearing.

"It's a promise," she grinned as she climbed out and put on her robe.

Raiden finally went home Sunday night, and when Elle's alarm went off Monday morning, she couldn't believe how empty her bed felt without him. It had only been one weekend.

Pushing the thought from her mind, she focused on getting her and Logan out the door.

She'd been at her desk for less than five minutes when her cell phone rang, and she smiled at the sight of Raiden's name on the screen.

"Good morning," she purred. Oh God, she actually purred. What had this man done to her?

"Good morning to you as well," he replied, and she could hear the grin in his voice. Elle couldn't help picturing the same boyish smirk that always made her stomach flutter.

"I missed you last night," she said, trying to sound…not turned on.

"You mean you weren't glad to have the whole bed back to yourself?" he asked.

"Not at all." She peeked at the door to make sure no one was close by and lowered her voice. "When do I get to have you back in it?"

"There is nothing I want more right now," he said, his own voice quiet. "But unfortunately that's why I'm calling."

"What's wrong?" she asked with a frown.

"Nothing wrong, per se," he said, speaking at a normal volume again. "I just came in this morning to find out that the trial date for one of my cases has been moved up to next week, so I'm going to be working overtime trying to make sure we're ready for it."

"Oh," she said, still frowning.

"You're pouting, aren't you?"

"What? No."

"Yes you are," he said. "I bet that tasty bottom lip of yours is sticking out right now," he said and she laughed. "But I understand. I'm pouting too."

"No, you're not," she said between giggles.

"You're right. I don't pout. But I am frowning. I was daydreaming my whole commute this morning about coming to see you after work."

"When will I get to see you again?"

"Not sure just yet. I promise to call when I can though."

"Hmm…we'll see if I can wait around long enough," she said playfully.

"That's just mean."

"I'm a busy woman."

"I know," he said. "But I promise to make it worth the wait."

"Now you're talking."

"I have to go, but I'll talk to you soon."

"Okay. Don't forget me," she said.

"Oh don't worry, I won't."

As Elle ended the call, she decided she was glad that she had been so selfish with Raiden this weekend.

By Thursday night the letters before Raiden's eyes were starting to blur together and he blinked a couple times, bringing them back into focus. There was some boring shit in this transcript, but unfortunately it was important shit, so he kept reading.

"Knock, knock."

He looked up to find Elle leaning against the doorway, a bag in her hand. He recognized the name of a nearby Italian restaurant stamped on the brown paper.

"What are you doing here?" he asked, feeling the smile slowly build on his face. There was no problem getting his eyes to focus now.

"I figured if you were anything like every other lawyer I know," she said, sauntering over to his desk—God, it was a turn-on just to watch her move— "then you rarely get to eat a decent meal in the middle of a big case."

He leaned back in his chair as she sat on the corner of his desk, setting the bag on the only clear space among all the files.

"Of that, I am guilty," he said and she leaned forward to give him a kiss.

"And I miss you," she said.

"I'm sorry."

"It's okay, I understand. That's why I decided to bring you dinner. You get to eat some real food, and I get to spend a few minutes with you."

"That's a great idea," he told her. "Where's Logan?

"I paid the nanny to stay late tonight."

"You didn't have to do that…."

"I know, but I wanted to."

He took a deep breath and his mouth watered at the scent of whatever was in the bag. "Is that lasagna I smell?" he asked.

"It is," she said and started pulling out boxes while Raiden made room for them on his desk.

He helped dish it up, and Elle pulled the extra chair around to his side so that their knees touched.

"This is amazing," he said. "Exactly what I needed."

"Glad I could help," she said.

Elle updated him on her work with the non-profit group as they ate, and then she surprised him again by pulling out dessert.

But all too soon they were taking the last bites of tiramisu.

"Well, I should probably let you get back to work," Elle said as she wiped her mouth.

"If you insist," Raiden sighed. "I can't wait for this case to be over."

"How much longer?" she asked, leaning on the desk and cupping her chin in her hand.

"If things go our way," he kissed her delicious mouth that was so close to him now, "only another week or so."

"And if they don't?"

"I don't even want to think about that right now," he said, shaking his head. "But we have a pretty strong case. I suspect that's why the defense fought so hard to move the trial up. They were hoping to catch us off guard."

"Then I need to get out of your hair so you can work on making things go your way." She stood and started gathering the trash.

"Let me help," he said, starting to stand, but she gently pushed him back down.

"You sit and get back to work. I can handle this." She grabbed the bag and started to walk out the door. "I'm going to put this in the break room garbage so it doesn't stink up your office overnight. Be right back."

"I miss you," he said before she was out the door.

She turned and gave him a heart-stopping smile. "I know."

Raiden stared at the neat pile of folders he had made so they wouldn't accidentally get food on them. Maybe with a full stomach he could focus better. But the truth was now he just wanted to crawl into bed. He looked up as Elle walked in, closing the door behind her and leaning against it. Specifically into bed with her.

"Do you know what?" she asked, still propped against the door with a playful look in her eyes. "We're the only ones here," she said, not waiting for him to answer. "Everyone else has left the office."

"Are you telling me that's my cue to leave the office and work from home?" he asked.

She walked over and gently pushed him and his

chair away from the desk. "Perhaps. But maybe not just yet."

He frowned for a split second until she straddled him and loosened his tie.

"Are you thinking what I'm thinking?" he asked, giving his own devilish smile.

"If I'm not, then there is something seriously wrong with you."

He laughed and pulled her face into his. He stopped a breath's distance from her face and she moved to close the distance, but he halted her.

"Weren't you just telling me I needed to get back to work?" he asked.

"Mmm…." She released his tie and slid her palms down his chest. "You're right. I should go."

Raiden gently slid her off his lap and stood before cupping her ass and lifting her onto the edge of his desk.

"I think we both know that's not going to happen now," he growled before slipping his tongue past her lips and she greeted him eagerly, wrapping her arms around his neck. He could feel her hands working on his belt, and then the zipper. Her skin was velvet against his mouth as he kissed along her chin, her throat, down to her delicate collarbone.

"I want you to fuck me," she breathed into his ear. "Right here on your desk."

"With pleasure," he murmured. He pulled off her top and traced the edge of her lace bra with his lips. She arched her back, thrusting her perfect breasts into him. After a quick check to make sure everything on the desk top had indeed been cleared away, he guided her to lay all the way back onto her elbows and undid her pants. She watched him hungrily as he pulled them off, leaving her naked ass to press against the polished wood of his desk. As he let the clothes drop, she sat back up and scooted to the very edge, pushing his pants and briefs down.

His breath hitched when her warm hand wrapped around his hard-on and her gray eyes stared into his own.

"How do you do that?" he whispered, placing both hands at the base of her back.

"Do what?" she asked with a giggle. "Give a hand job?"

"No. How do you stare into my soul like that?"

Her expression softened, as though something were melting away, though what, he didn't know. Without answering his question, Elle used her grip on him to guide him closer, and he watched her eyes close as he slid into her.

"Oh God," she moaned, opening them again to smile at him.

He kissed the corner of her mouth and she shifted

her head to nibble on his ear. His knees had never felt so weak. Her hands slid around to his back and gently scraped their way up as he slid out and thrust into her again, harder this time, drawing his name from her lips. He never knew hearing his own name could be so intoxicating.

He slammed into her again, and this time the whole desk moved. He didn't care though, as he quickened his movements. He'd chase it across the room if he had to.

Elle moved her arms up to around his neck, bringing her face close to his. He could see the heat spreading across her cheeks, the sheen of sweat glistening on her forehead. And then her eyes closed and she was biting her lip. Raiden picked up the pace, tightening his grip around her, and she was coming around him. It was all he could do to hold off his own climax as he tried to keep hers going. But then she wrapped her legs around him so hard, he had no choice but to let go.

When it was done, he dropped his hands to the desk on either side of her, burying his face into her shoulder. She clung to his neck, as though afraid she would fall off. After a couple breaths, he lifted his face to see her look of complete satisfaction.

"Thank you, Mr. Kane," she said breathlessly.

"Thank *you*," he replied with a smile. She

released him and he was just able to pull his pants back up before falling back into his chair. "I have to say, I don't think I'll ever be able to look at my desk again without remembering this."

She hopped off the desk and started stepping back into her own pants before climbing onto his lap.

"At least now I know you won't forget about me whenever you're working those late hours," she said as Raiden caressed her still naked back.

"Was never possible," he said, looking up into her steel-colored eyes, "but I appreciate the effort."

"I should get going and really let you get back to work this time," she said.

"I'll walk you out. It's clear I'm not going to be very productive here, thinking about what we just did...*here*."

She giggled and he kissed her. When did he get so lucky?

Six

It was Thursday afternoon again a couple weeks later, and Raiden was about to call it a day when his cell phone rang.

"Hi, Mom," he said as he started slipping files into his bag.

"Hi, Sweetie. Did I catch you at a bad time?" his mother asked.

"For you, Mom, it's never a bad time," he said with a grin.

"So long as you answer the phone," she shot back.

Raiden shrugged. "Comes with the territory of my job, I suppose." He heard the familiar sigh from the other end. The proud sigh. Judy Kane's son was an attorney. "What's up?" he asked.

"I just wanted to check that you were still okay with picking me up from the train station tomorrow at five. If it's too early, I'll just take a cab to your apartment and wait."

Raiden stopped what he was doing. How could he have forgotten his mom was coming this weekend? Elle's dad and step-mom were taking Logan to the Mariner's baseball game tomorrow night, so he'd made dinner reservations for Friday.

"Are you still there?" Judy asked. "Are you sure I'm not interrupting anything?"

"No, it's fine," he said, sitting down in his chair. "Of course I'll pick you up tomorrow. And while you're here, there's someone I'd like you to meet."

"Oh, really? Have you started dating already?"

"I—I have actually."

"Is she nice?"

"No, Mom, she's absolutely horrid," he replied, rolling his eyes.

"That's not what I mean. I just…I just don't want to see you get hurt again."

"I know. And I promise you she's not Maureen. Her name is Elle, and," he couldn't stop the grin from forming on his face, "and she's amazing."

"Then I can't wait to meet her. See you tomorrow, Sweetie. I love you."

"Love you too, Mom," he said. "See you tomorrow."

As Raiden headed down to the parking garage, he called El Gaucho to add one more person to the reservation and then called Elle to make sure she was ready to meet his mother. Hell, Raiden wasn't even sure *he* was ready for them to meet.

Elle's phone rang just as she walked in the door, and she grinned when Raiden's name popped up on the screen.

"Hey, Sexy."

"Hey, Gorgeous," he replied, and her smile got that much bigger. "I need to talk to you about tomorrow night."

"You're not canceling on me?" she asked, feeling the smile melt from her face. "I was so looking forward to a grown-up night out with you."

"No, we're still on for tomorrow night. But we'll have company."

"Company?" she asked, trying to hide her disappointment.

"I kind of forgot that my mom was coming up this weekend."

"How could you forget something like that?"

"I don't know. For some reason I didn't put it in my calendar, and so of course it slipped my mind.

But it wouldn't feel right leaving her home alone when she's only here for two nights."

"I completely understand. I don't have to come along if you don't want to. Technically you had plans with her first."

"Of course I want you to join me. Unless you don't want to meet my mother. If it's too soon—"

"Raiden," she said, cutting him off. "I would love to meet your mother."

"Are you sure?"

"Absolutely. How else am I going to find out what kind of troublemaker you were as a child?" she asked with a giggle. But he gave a nervous laugh. "What's the matter?" she asked, half serious. "Afraid of what she might say?"

"Oh, I can just imagine the embarrassing stories my mother would love to tell," he said, and she couldn't help but sense his discomfort.

"Don't worry," she assured him. "I promise not to pry…much. Besides, I'm sure my dad will share my own horror stories soon enough."

"Should I pick you up at six-thirty?" he asked. "The reservation is for seven."

"You don't have to drag your mom out here and then back. The restaurant is so close to you, I'll just meet you guys there."

"Are you sure? I don't mind, and I'm sure she

won't either."

"Logan will be home around ten, and it's not like you'll be spending the night."

"True," he sighed. "See you tomorrow night then."

Elle was the first to arrive at the restaurant on Friday night, but she had only just sat down on the bench by the hostess' booth when Raiden walked in with his mother. Raiden was dressed in his usual weekend clothes—button-down shirt and designer jeans—but while his mother was dressed in similar fashion, it couldn't have been a starker contrast to her son's outfit. Judy's shirt, while also a button-down, was faded and had a generic floral pattern on it. Her jeans were ill-fitting and equally faded.

Elle stood and took Judy's hand in hers, wanting to make a good impression.

"You must be Raiden's mother," she said and watched the smile light up her face.

"And you must be Elle. It's so nice to meet you," she said, grasping Elle's hand with both of hers. "Raiden has been telling me all about you on the way over."

Elle blushed and looked from Raiden to his mother, finding only the faintest traces of her in him.

It made her that much more curious to know what his father had looked like. She also saw the face of a beautiful woman that life had not been kind to. There were lines around her eyes that Elle imagined came with territory when one had to raise a son on her own.

"Right this way," a hostess announced, cutting through Elle's thoughts, and she tried to mentally shake the judgments she was forming in her mind. Raiden had explained more than once that they had not grown up with money, but as he stood here next to his mother, Elle felt she was seeing the before and after of Raiden.

Raiden let the two women slide into the booth opposite each other before moving in next to Elle.

"How was your trip up here, Ms. Kane?" Elle asked.

"Oh, please, call me Judy," she said. "And it was good. I usually take the train up from Portland. Have you ever done that before?"

"I haven't," Elle told her. "But I hear it's a beautiful journey. Probably more relaxing than driving the three hours."

"Maybe one day we could take it down to go visit my mom," Raiden said, smiling at Elle.

"Only if we were invited, of course," Elle said, looking back to Judy.

"Raiden knows he's invited any time. He could show up at my door unannounced and I'd still be thrilled."

"What mom wouldn't, right?"

"Raiden tells me you have a son as well," said Judy.

"I do. Logan. He's four."

"That's such a fun age. Right before they start school when everything changes." She gave a Raiden a knowing look before continuing. "Who's watching him tonight?"

"He's at a baseball game with my dad. He'll be dropped off later tonight," Elle explained.

"That's nice that you have family close and willing to help."

"Absolutely. They've definitely been a lifesaver for me," said Elle. "Do you get down to California to see your family very often?" Elle asked, and there was a definite shift in mood not only with Judy, but also with Raiden, who stiffened next to her.

"There isn't much family left down there," he said.

"No one worth seeing," his mother muttered.

"Oh." Elle wasn't sure how to respond to that. But Raiden was quick to steer the conversation.

"So Mom, Elle works for a tutoring company, but you should hear about this amazing program she's working on."

Elle couldn't help but smile at him as she heard the pride in his voice. She spent the next ten minutes telling Judy about her pet project, and without any more mention of their family, everyone stayed in good spirits throughout dinner.

If Raiden was completely honest with himself, he'd been nervous about his mom and Elle meeting each other. Thankfully, his fears had been unwarranted—the two seemed to get along just fine. The conversation all through dinner was light but easygoing. And when Elle excused herself to use the restroom as they were all pushing away their nearly empty plates, he could almost breathe a sigh of relief.

"That was delicious," said his mom, giving her stomach a pat.

"I'm glad you enjoyed it," he said, giving her a big smile.

"So are we here because you're trying to impress me or her?"

"What are you talking about?" he asked.

"In all the times I've come up to visit, you've never brought me somewhere this fancy."

"Well, I should've. You deserve it, Mom," he said with a smile. But her expression remained serious. "And things like this don't impress Elle," he added.

"I don't doubt that," she said. "I see the way she carries herself, how comfortable she is in a place like this. How did you two meet, anyway?"

Raiden leaned back and went to put an arm over the back of the seat but had forgotten how high it was. He dropped both hands into his lap instead.

"Elle's father happens to be my boss, Marcus Williams. She and I met at a company event. And yes, it's true that she was raised with money. But she doesn't care about stuff like that."

"Of course not. She's never had to go without. Probably never had to wonder how she was going to make rent, or feed her son."

"What is it you're trying to say?" he asked with a frown. "Do you not like Elle?"

"I do like her. She's seems nice, and it's obvious she cares about you. You're the one that I'm worried about."

Raiden raised an eyebrow. "Me?"

"Does she know about California?"

"She knows that's where I grew up."

"I see. And so you've told her why we moved away?"

"No," he said, unable to meet her gaze. "It's not important."

"It's not important?" she asked in a tone that demanded he look her in the eye. "Or you think she won't stick around if she knew the truth?"

"It's not important," he repeated. "It's in the past and there's no point in bringing it up."

Her brow wrinkled as she frowned slightly.

"If you care about her as much as you say you do," she said, "then you should tell her. And if you don't think she'll see you the same way once she knows, well then—"

"Not now, Mom." Raiden could see Elle making her way back to the booth. Even if his mom was right, this was not the time nor place to have that conversation.

"I'm just saying," his mom muttered as Elle slid in next to him.

"Anyone ready to order dessert?" Raiden asked, forcing a smile.

"I don't know if I could eat another bite," said Elle.

"I think I'm full too," said Judy.

Raiden paid the bill and the three of them migrated to the sidewalk outside the restaurant.

"Do you have anything exciting planned for tomorrow?" Elle asked while they waited for valet to bring her car around.

"I don't think so," his mother said, looking at him.

"I'm sure we'll find something to explore," he told her.

"Although I was reading about this Museum of Flight in a magazine on the way up here," said Judy. "Have you heard of it?"

Raiden looked at Elle. "That's the one by Boeing Field, isn't it?" he asked, and she nodded. "It's settled then. We're going to the Museum of Flight tomorrow."

"It looks like a great place for kids," his mother offered to Elle. "You and your little boy should join us."

"I bet Logan would love it. But only if we weren't imposing." She gave Raiden a questioning look.

"The more the merrier," he said just as her Volvo pulled up to the curb.

"Great," said Elle, giving him a chaste kiss on the cheek. "Shoot me a text when you decide when we should head over. Good night, Judy. It was a pleasure meeting you."

"Same to you, dear. See you tomorrow."

Raiden and his mom walked toward the direction of his apartment as she drove off.

"Should we watch a movie tonight?" he asked,

offering his arm to her.

"A movie sounds nice, Sweetie," she said, hooking her left arm through and patting him with her other hand. "Sorry for ruining your plans."

"What are you talking about? You didn't ruin my plans."

"I can't imagine dinner was all you had planned with that gorgeous woman."

Raiden laughed even as he felt himself blush. "Way to be subtle, Mom," he said, and she laughed with him. "Way to be subtle."

Logan was just as excited about the museum as Elle had imagined. Waiting in line to buy their tickets was almost too much for him, and he took off running as they approached the expansive open space full of aircrafts of all shapes, sizes, and vintages.

"Logan!" Elle called out.

"Don't worry, I got him," Raiden said as he headed after him. Raiden's long stride quickly caught up with Logan's short little legs, and the two of them walked down the stairs hand in hand.

"Can I just say that my son adores your son?" Judy commented as the two of them sauntered in their direction.

Elle smiled. "They're two peas in a pod, aren't

they?"

"Please don't break his heart."

Elle came to a sudden stop and looked at Judy, who also halted. "What?"

"It's good to see him happy, especially after what that awful woman did to him. But I don't think his heart could handle any more heartbreak. No matter how tough he may seem."

Judy was staring out at Raiden down on the main exhibit floor, and Elle could see a saddened, almost wistful expression on her face.

"You're not just referring to his divorce, are you?" Elle asked softly.

Judy's worry lines deepened.

"Do you mind if I ask about Raiden's father?"

"He hasn't told you?" Judy asked, finally tearing her eyes from her son.

"He told me that he died of a heart attack."

"It was...hard on him." Judy looked disapprovingly at Raiden, which confused Elle. "Leaving California was the best thing we ever did."

There was a definite bitterness in her voice. Elle could only imagine how painful the memories had been.

"So from one mother to another," said Judy, "please take care of my son."

"I will," Elle promised.

"Thank you." Judy gave her a warm smile, and Elle knew she spoke out of concern for her son.

Without warning, Logan slammed into Elle's legs. She hadn't even seen him coming and was almost knocked over.

"Careful, Sweetie," she said, regaining her balance.

"Sorry Mommy."

"What's taking you slowpokes so long?" Raiden asked as he caught up to them with a huge grin on his face.

"Sorry," she said, mustering a smile. "We got distracted."

Raiden's smile faltered and he looked from her to his mother, then back again. "Is everything okay?"

"Of course it is," she said and gave him a quick kiss. "Lead the way."

Once Logan was convinced he had seen every nook and cranny of the museum (Elle decided not to tell him there was a whole second building across the sky bridge) he let them drag him out to Raiden's car.

"I think someone is going to fall asleep on the way home," Elle said as she climbed into the back seat next to Logan, already strapped into his car seat.

"Not Logan," Raiden called from the driver's seat. "You won't fall asleep on me, will you, little man?"

Logan shook his head as a huge yawn stretched across his face, causing all the grown-ups to laugh.

Seven

On Sunday afternoon, Elle was on the floor of her living room doing a puzzle with Logan when the doorbell rang.

"This is a welcome surprise," she said as she opened the door for Raiden. The way his face lit up at the sight of her set off the butterflies in her stomach.

"I just dropped my mom off and thought I would swing by and see if you and Logan would be interested in joining me for lunch."

"That sounds like a great idea," she said. "What did you have in mind?"

"There's a new place that just opened in the University Village. And I even checked on the way here to make sure they had a kid's menu."

"Welcome to my world," she muttered.

The three of them piled into Elle's car rather than transfer the car seat and crossed the Montlake Bridge to the University District, an area that included not only the expansive University of Washington campus, but a whole thriving community with an outdoor shopping complex on the outskirts of the neighborhood.

Halfway through lunch, Raiden escorted Logan to the bathroom, leaving Elle at the table. She was about to take a bite of her sandwich when she heard an oddly familiar laughter carrying over from a nearby table. Elle looked around for its source, sure that it was just a coincidence. But when her eyes landed on the woman who had laughed again, Elle's stomach tightened.

Not even really aware of what she was doing, she stood and wound her way through the tables.

"Mom?"

The woman looked up, startled, and then recognition dawned across her face. "Oh my God, Ellie? What are you doing here?"

Ellie. She had forgotten Blair was the only one who ever called her that.

"I live here, remember?" said Elle. "What are *you* doing here?"

"I, um…" Blair looked at the teenager sitting across from her, and Elle finally took notice of the girl. "We're visiting the local college campuses," she said, turning back to Elle. "This is my step-daughter. She'll be a senior in high school next year."

Elle felt like someone had punched her in the gut. She had been crazy to imagine Blair, all these years, sitting sad and alone, pining over the family she had walked away from, the daughter she no longer knew.

And then Logan was wrapping his arms around her knees and time started moving for her again. She could hear the voices all around her, the clatter of dishes.

"Sorry about that," Raiden said, scooping Logan into his arms. "He got away from me as we came back out. Hi, I'm Raiden."

Elle gave a strange little laugh. He thought this was a friendly run-in.

"Is this your family?" she asked without a trace of emotion.

"Yes," Elle said rather forcefully, before Raiden tried to explain.

"Oh."

"This is your grandson," Elle whispered, and she heard Raiden's gasp from beside her.

"Let's go back to the table and finish our lunch," he said to Logan, and they walked away.

Blair stood and spoke quietly to Elle. "What exactly is it that you want from me?"

"An explanation," Elle said, frowning.

Blair looked over Elle's shoulder, and then back at her. "You have a beautiful family over there. Why don't you go back to them and let me get back to mine?"

Elle was speechless as Blair sat back down in her chair. The step-daughter awkwardly averted her eyes. Elle turned and slowly walked back to the table.

"Are you alright?" Raiden asked when she sat down.

She could only nod.

"Are you sure you're okay?" Raiden asked when they walked into Elle's house, and again she nodded. But it was obvious that she wasn't, and Raiden was feeling helpless.

He watched her sink into the couch and grab the remote, but she just sat there, not actually hitting the power button.

"Hey, Logan," Raiden said, "can you go play in your room for a minute while I talk to your mom?"

"Okay."

Logan trudged up the stairs and Raiden sat on the couch next to Elle. He took the remote from her hand and pulled her into him, where she heaved a big sigh against his chest.

"Was I that awful of a daughter—"

"Oh, Elle—"

"—that she had to go find a new family?"

"You know that's not true."

She sat up to look at him, and her eyes were full of tears. "Then why do people keep leaving me?" She choked on the last word, blinking back the tears that threatened to fall.

"It's them, Elle. This has nothing to do with you." She buried her face into his chest again, and he rubbed her back. "You have your father and Jeannie. They love you, Elle. And you have me," he said, stalling on the words he really wanted to say. He settled on, "I'm not going anywhere."

She sat up, wiping her face with her hands. "You're right, I'm sorry."

"What are you sorry for?" he asked with a frown.

"Because there's no point in being sad over people like…them. Not when I have the right people in my life."

"I didn't mean you can't be sad—"

"I know," she said. "But I have more important things to do today, like spending time with you and Logan."

He smiled and kissed the corner of her mouth.

"And what would you like to do today?"

"Let's take Logan to the park. I think he and I could use some fresh air."

"Sounds like a great idea to me."

Elle climbed off the couch, calling Logan, and Raiden watched from where he continued to sit. He didn't know why Elle's mom had left all those years ago, or why Logan's dad was such a deadbeat. But they were all missing out, and he was never going to let Elle feel abandoned again.

First thing Monday morning Raiden rapped on the open door of Marcus' office.

"Do you have a minute," he said when Marcus looked up.

"I have five," said Marcus. "What's up?"

Raiden stepped in and closed the door part-way behind him.

"We ran into Elle's mother yesterday."

"Blair?" Marcus gasped. "What's she doing in town?"

"I'm not sure, sir," Raiden told him. "Elle isn't saying much about it."

"How's Elle taking it?"

Raiden sat in the chair facing Marcus' desk, unsure how much to tell Elle's father.

"She seems fine now, but she was pretty rattled

by it. She wonders why her mother went and found herself a new family."

Marcus leaned back in his own chair with a heavy sigh.

"Was Blair there with someone else?" he asked. "Or did she say something to Elle?"

"She was there with her step-daughter."

"I see," Marcus said, nodding slightly. "What has Elle told you about Blair?"

"Only that you two split up when she was ten. That she saw her mother from time to time after that, and then…nothing. To be honest, I didn't even know her name until yesterday."

"Blair was—is still perhaps—a woman who was never quite sure what she wanted, but knew it wasn't what she had. Looking back now, it was a miracle that she stuck with us for as long as she did. And when I told her she couldn't just keep drifting in and out of Elle's life whenever she saw fit, Blair happily walked away. Said it was one less responsibility to worry about. As if she had too many of them." There was no mistaking the bitterness in Marcus' voice. "I know she remarried and divorced again by the time I stopped keeping tabs on her—when I realized there was nothing Elle and I could have done differently. Who knows, maybe this current family is finally giving her the peace she's been looking for all these years."

There was a knock on the door, and Cassie popped her blonde head in.

"Your nine o'clock is here," she said.

"I'll be out in a minute," Marcus told her and she disappeared again. "Thank you for telling me, Raiden. And you will let me know if she is still struggling with this?"

"Of course, sir."

They both stood and were almost to the door when Marcus spoke again.

"I'm glad she has you to look out for her. And Logan."

"Thank you," said Raiden, floored by the compliment. "They mean a lot to me."

Raiden walked in to Elle's office the next evening to find her on the phone. She flashed him a smile as he sat down in the chair across from her.

"All right, thank you," she said and hung up the phone before leaning across the desk on her forearms. "This is a pleasant surprise."

"I just got done with a meeting nearby," he said, "and wanted to see if you and Logan were available for dinner?"

"Wow," she looked at the clock, "I didn't realize it was that late already. Logan should be dropped off soon. Where did you have in mind?"

"Zeke's again?"

"Logan'll like that," she said with a smile. "I think that's his favorite place, thanks to you."

"I'm honored."

"He's pretty smitten with you."

"The feeling's mutual. That's a pretty awesome kid you got there." He leaned across the desk until their faces were only inches from each other. "And I think his mom is pretty hot too."

She closed the gap between them and they enjoyed a long, slow kiss before footsteps down the hall forced them back to a respectable distance.

"There's the little man," Raiden said as Logan walked in with the nanny.

"Raiden!" he yelled as he wrapped his arms around Raiden's legs.

"Thanks, Missy. See you tomorrow," Elle said to the nanny as Raiden picked up Logan and positioned him on his hip. It was amazing how natural this felt.

The three of them walked to the pizza parlor, where Logan begged Raiden to play tic tac toe with him again as soon as they were seated. He still let Logan win most of the games, but he decided it might be good to let him lose a couple as well.

As the meal was winding down, the server came over with the check.

"Is there anything else I can get you guys before I leave this here?" she asked.

"Ice cream!" Logan cried out.

The server laughed. "You'll have to talk to your mom and dad about that."

Raiden and Elle looked at each, almost horrified.

"Raiden," Logan said, turning to him. "Can I have chocolate ice cream?"

"Uh," he looked at Elle, who, surprisingly, was stifling a giggle. She gave a slight nod. "Sure, why not?"

"Chocolate ice cream it is," said the server before turning to leave.

"Why did you ask me instead of your mom?" Raiden asked Logan, who had turned his attention back to coloring.

"Because mommy would've said no," he answered.

"I told you," said Elle.

After dinner, Raiden walked Elle and Logan to her car, where he helped strap Logan into the booster seat.

"See ya later, little man," he said to Logan, who gave him the biggest grin.

"Bye bye, Raiden."

Raiden turned to Elle who had her own smile for

him—only this one was much more seductive.

"Are you coming over tonight?" she asked as she wrapped her arms around his neck.

"I would love to," he said, wrapping his own arms around her waist, pulling her into him. "But I have so much work to do tonight."

She frowned. "You could always bring it over."

"Not sure I would get much done with you around," he said, grinning, but she only responded by pouting even more. "Stick that bottom lip out any more," he whispered, "and I just might have to bite it."

She finally smiled and he kissed her.

"Are you sure?" she asked as they pulled apart.

"If I didn't have to be in London next week, I would. But as it is—"

"Wait, you're going to London?" she asked, frowning again.

"Did I not mention it?"

"No. What are you going to London for?"

"I'm attending an international law conference. Are you sure I didn't mention it?"

"I think I would have remembered. When are you leaving?"

"I leave this Sunday and get back the following Friday."

Elle lowered her hands and rested them on his

chest. "I guess I should let you go then," she sighed.

"What are you guys doing this weekend? I still want to…," he glanced over at Logan, who was happily singing a new song he must've learned at preschool today. "I still want to *see* you before I leave," he whispered.

The corners of her mouth went up as she decoded his meaning. "As it happens," she said, "Logan is spending the weekend at my dad's."

"Well in that case," he said with a smile on his face. "Why don't you come spend the weekend at my place?"

"That sounds perfect," she said and gave him one last kiss before getting into her car and driving off.

As Raiden walked back to his apartment, it was hard to keep the stupid grin off of his face. It was incredible to think how far he had come since those days back in California. He loved his job, had a great apartment in the middle of a beautiful city, and was about to spend the weekend with the sexiest, most amazing woman he had ever met. Life was good.

The Green Room was only half full when Elle and Raiden sat down to a small table in the back of the bar's lower level.

"So you know this band?" she asked, gesturing to the guys setting up on the tiny stage near the stairwell.

"I don't know them personally," he said. "I just used to go to their shows a lot when I was growing up in California. After all these years, it's nice to see them doing out-of-state venues, albeit still small ones." He took a sip of beer. "I want to show my support."

"That's so sweet," said Elle.

"No it's not," he said, trying to look offended by the word 'sweet.'

"Admit it, Raiden," she said, draping an arm around his shoulder and nuzzling into his ear. "You're just a big softie."

He turned to kiss her. "Only for you."

"Raiden?" A strange man's voice cut into their intimate moment. "Raiden Kane? Is that really you?"

Elle looked up to see a rough-looking man with tattoos everywhere, including his knuckles and a couple creeping up his neck, and—it was hard to tell in the poor lighting—she thought she could make out a teardrop shape near the corner of his left eye. He was clearly ecstatic to have run into Raiden, but Raiden's smile did not match the newcomer's, and just like when they had gone to dinner with his mom, she felt his whole body tense up.

She pulled her arm from his shoulder and took his hand under the table. He gave it a hard squeeze.

"Roger, what are you doing here?" he asked.

"Aw, man, don't be so formal. Call me Roach."

"Still going by that moniker, I see."

Roach looked confused.

"I said I see you are still going by that nickname."

"Why wouldn't I?"

"So what are you doing in Seattle?" asked Raiden.

"My baby sister moved up here a few years ago and now she's getting married tomorrow. To some fancy tech guy, can you believe it? The guy's a fucking prick though. But you should see his house—he's got some nice shit, I tell you."

Raiden nodded as he took another swig of beer, choosing not to comment.

"Who's your lady friend?" Roach asked with a smile that was borderline leering, and Raiden gave her hand another firm squeeze.

"This is my girlfriend, Elle. Elle, this is Roach. We used to hang out together in California."

"Nice to meet you," she said.

"You too. Mind if I join you guys?" he asked.

"Be our guest," said Raiden, motioning to an empty seat. Elle knew this man was the last person Raiden wanted with them, but he wasn't about to be so rude.

"Benny's here too," Roach said, taking the seat. "He's upstairs grabbing some drinks, but he'll be real surprised to see you."

"How long are you guys in town for?" asked Raiden.

"Benny and me have to drive back down on Monday."

"That's a shame," said Raiden as he polished off his bottle. Elle decided it might be better if she didn't order a second cocktail.

"I still can't believe I ran into you here. Last I heard you were still in Oregon. Eugene was it?"

Raiden gave a nod. "My mom's still there, but it was too small for me."

Elle wondered why Raiden would lie about where his mom was living.

"Whatcha up to these days?" Roach asked.

"This and that," said Raiden. "Keeping my nose clean."

"I hear ya," said Roach. "Looking at my third strike next time."

Elle almost spit out her drink. He couldn't seriously mean "prison-for-life" third strike, could he? How did Raiden know these people?

"Better be careful, Roach."

Roach's friend Benny finally arrived and there was the same excitement as before, but again, not as much enthusiasm coming from Raiden.

The music finally started up and talking was impossible. A couple songs in. Elle had to pee, but she was reluctant to leave Raiden alone. When she felt ready to burst, she whispered into his ear where she was going and headed to the bathrooms.

By the time she came out, the band had taken a break and Raiden looked pissed.

"Didn't you tell the babysitter you would be back by ten?" he said before she had even sat back down.

"Um, yeah." She looked at her watch, knowing that Raiden must have reached his breaking point. "We should get going, huh?"

"You got kids?" asked Benny.

"Elle does," said Raiden, standing up, "and I need to get her home to relieve the sitter."

"It was nice meeting you," said Elle. "Good luck with your sister's wedding."

"Thanks," said Roach, winking at her, and she resisted the urge to shudder. He turned to Raiden, who was helping Elle into her sweater. "And you should come down and visit sometime. If you ever need work, you know Big Joe would be happy to hook you up." There was a definite pause from Raiden, and Elle thought he was shaking when he finally moved again.

"I told you I'm trying to stay out of trouble," he

said. "And you would be smart to do the same thing."

"What's the matter, Raiden?" asked Roach, and Elle knew the mood had shifted. "Think you're too good for us?"

"Just trying to stay out of prison," said Raiden, and he pushed Elle in front of him and up the stairs to the front door.

"Who were those men?" Elle asked as soon as they stepped out onto the sidewalk.

"I told you, they're just some guys I used to hang out with." Raiden took her hand and tried to pull her in the direction of his apartment.

But she yanked it out of his grip. "Then why are you so spooked? What is going on?"

"Fine. I'll tell you everything. But let's get back to my place first." He gave a nervous glance towards the club's entrance and held out his hand. "I don't think they'll try and follow us, but just in case."

Raiden unlocked the door and let Elle enter first. The hall lamp was the only light on, and he watched her silhouette disappear into the kitchen but didn't immediately follow. After all his hard work, was it about to disappear because of a chance encounter? Not only the woman he cared about, but his job because her father happened to be his employer?

He reminded himself that he had never lied, never taken any shortcuts. He deserved to be here as much as any of them. Now he just needed to convince Elle.

"Raiden," she said, stepping back into the hall.

"Coming."

They sat down at the kitchen island, and Raiden took one of her hands in both of his. The granite felt colder than usual against his bottom hand, and a slight shiver swept through him.

"First of all," he started, "I need you to understand that Roach and Benny are from my past. A past that I have worked very hard to forget. I never thought in a million years that I would ever see them again. I had *hoped* that I would never see them."

"They're gang members, aren't they?" she asked.

"Yes."

"Were *you* in their gang?"

He nodded, and she gasped.

"I don't believe it," she said.

Raiden pulled down his shirt to reveal the scar she had noticed before. "I told you this was my first tattoo. It was the gang's insignia."

"But how do you go from being a gang member to being a successful attorney?" She waved her hand around the luxury apartment. "To all of this? I mean, how did you even get into law school?"

He tried not to take offense at her last question.

"After my father died, I didn't handle it well and eventually found myself hanging with a rough crowd. Before I knew it, I was on a very dangerous path and who knows where I would be right now if it hadn't been for a juvenile lawyer who gave me a chance to start over. Certainly not here with you," he said, giving her a weak smile that she didn't return. He searched her face for clues to what was going through her mind right now. Disbelief for sure, but he thought he saw concern in there as well. He tried to tell himself it was a good sign that she hadn't walked out the door yet, that she was giving him a chance to explain.

"Moreno's wasn't as hardcore as you might be imagining, but it still involved illegal activities— including a chop shop and distribution of pot."

"Did you smoke it?" she asked.

"I tried it once," he said.

"Even I've done that," she said with a laugh that helped to relieve some of Raiden's anxiety. "What did you do then?" she asked. "Were you a drug dealer?"

"No. I boosted cars."

Her eyes went wide. "You were a car thief?"

"I was pretty good at it, until I got busted in a sting. That's where Geoff Sutnick comes in. Before him, I hated lawyers and cops. I thought they were all a bunch of—well, I didn't think too highly of them. But Sutnick took the time to get to know me and worked with me to get a plea bargain. Time served, some community service, and it would be expunged on my eighteenth birthday, which was only six months away.

"He gave me a fresh start and my mother didn't want to see it go to waste, so she moved us to Eugene to keep me from falling back in with the same crowd. And despite my lack of effort, school came easy to me. After graduation I went to community college while working full time and applying for every scholarship I could find. Eventually I transferred into Oregon State.

"The whole time, I knew it wouldn't have been possible without Sutnick's legal help. I decided to go into law and managed to get into the University of Washington's law school. Just barely, but I graduated magna cum laude."

"And yet you went to work at a prominent law firm," she said. "How does that help troubled youth?"

"You work for an upscale tutoring company, yet what has been your greatest accomplishment there?"

She blushed. "The mentoring program," she whispered.

"Being at your father's firm has enabled me to do the most good. I happen to have the most pro bono hours of anyone there. And I still came out with a small amount of student loans that I have since paid off in full. And last year I bought my mom a house. The first home she has ever owned."

"In Eugene?"

"No," he said. "I lied about that, just in case."

Elle nodded but said nothing more. Raiden was hopeful, though, because during the whole conversation, Elle had not pulled her hand from his grasp. Not once.

Eight

"Are you going to tell me what you're thinking?" Raiden finally asked Elle as she tried to process everything he had just told her.

"Does my father know?" was the first question that she could come up with. Because she couldn't help but wonder why he never said anything if he knew.

"That I was in a gang? No. Outside of California, you're now that only other person that knows besides my mother."

"Not even Maureen?"

"Not even her."

"May I ask why?"

"Because it's something that I've tried to forget.

Because the truth is that I couldn't trust her with something like this."

"I see," Elle said, nodding.

"I would never ask you to lie to your father," he said. "But I would rather that he didn't know about my past."

"Why?" asked Elle. "You've already worked this long for him. Do you really think he would fire you if he found out?"

"I don't know. I'm just not sure I want to risk it. If he were to let me go because of it, I might not be able to get another job if he told the next person."

She shook her head. "I think you're wrong about him. But I understand."

"Does that mean you're okay with it then?"

With her free hand, she turned his right arm over and touched where she knew his tattoo was beneath the sleeve of his shirt.

"Is this what you meant about remembering what path you're on?"

He nodded.

"I have to admit that if I had known this from the beginning," she said with a frown, "then I might never had made it this far with you." She looked up into his eyes. "And now I know that would have been a mistake."

She leaned forward and gently pressed her lips

against his. He released her hand and held her face as he kissed her back.

Their lips parted and she pushed back the sleeve of his shirt, exposing the compass on his forearm, and kissed the tattoo.

"I'm glad you found your way to me," she said as she stood and pulled him with her in the direction of the bedroom.

"Do you remember when I said you were different," she asked as she started undressing him, "and you wondered if that was a good thing?"

"Yes," he whispered as he began doing the same to her.

"The answer is yes. Because different is exactly what I needed."

She backed up on to the bed and he followed, climbing atop her, and she pulled his face down to hers so she could fill his mouth with her tongue.

"I love you, Raiden," she mumbled between kisses.

He paused, locking eyes with her, and Elle worried she had said the wrong words.

"I love you too, Elle. More than you could possibly know."

When Raiden woke the next morning with Elle's legs tangled up in his, he felt like a weight had been lifted from his shoulders. She knew the truth about his messy past and she was still here with him. Not only that, but she had told him that she loved him.

A deep, contented sigh escaped Elle's lip as she slept and Raiden smiled, wondering what she was dreaming about. All he wanted to do today was stay right here, tangled up in her beautiful naked body.

But then the alarm on his cell phone went off, reminding him that he had a plane to catch in a couple hours.

Elle stirred but didn't wake yet, and Raiden was reluctant to disturb her blissful slumber, so he carefully slid out of bed and got in the shower. He hadn't been under the hot water for more than a minute when he heard the shower door open. Elle was wrapped her arms around him from behind.

"Good morning," he said as he turned around.

"Morning. Do you have to leave soon?"

He nodded.

"This is going to be a long week," she sighed.

"Tell me about it," he said. "You won't forget about me, will you?"

She grinned. "Not a chance."

"But just in case…." He pressed his mouth to her throat as he gently pushed her against one of the shower walls. He was going to give her a shower experience she would always remember.

It was breakfast time for most of London as Raiden walked into the room of his hotel. Registration at the conference didn't open until after lunch, and he was hoping to get a nap in beforehand. But first….

He rolled his suitcase over to the closet and sat on the edge of the bed, pulling his cell phone from his inside jacket pocket.

The tone was different as he made the international call, but it connected all the same.

"Hello," said Elle's groggy voice on the other end.

"I'm sorry, did I wake you?" he asked.

"No…I mean, yes, but it's fine. What time is it there?"

"It's nine. In the morning. I didn't think about the time difference. I can call you back later," he said.

"No, it's good to hear your voice," she said. "Are you at your hotel yet?"

"Sitting in my room right now. Wishing you were here with me."

"Mmm, me too."

"This is my first time out of the country, you know," he told her.

"Is it really? How sad that you had to go by

yourself."

"I know, right? Next time I'll have to bring you with me."

"I would like that," she purred.

"I should let you go back to sleep," he said. "I just wanted to call you."

"I'm glad you did. It's going to be a long week without you."

He smiled at her words but said, "You survived plenty of weeks without me before you and I met."

"Yes, but now I know what I'm missing."

"Same here," he said. "Now go back to sleep. I'll call again when I get a chance. And I'll figure out the time difference before then."

"I love you," she said.

"I love you too, Elle. Sweet dreams."

Raiden's call the day he landed in London proved to be his only chance due to his busy schedule and the time difference. But Elle woke every morning to texts, some sweet, some just downright naughty, and some accompanied by pictures of him in front of various landmarks he encountered throughout his day.

He clearly did not like to smile when taking pictures of himself—even apologized for the lack of them—but Elle didn't mind. She loved the smoldering gazes he inadvertently sent across the ocean more anyway. She often found herself flipping through the photos whenever she had a moment to herself. Friday afternoon could not come soon enough.

In an effort not to go stir-crazy the last night without Raiden, Elle headed to her father's house, where she and Logan had dinner.

It was getting late by the time she excused Logan from the table, but Elle was in no hurry to get back to her empty bed. She watched Logan as he disappeared into the room where bins of trains were stored. That should buy her a little time.

"Are you excited for Raiden to come home tomorrow?" her father asked as though reading her thoughts.

"Maybe a little," she said with a sly smile. "I barely even noticed his absence."

"Liar," her father laughed.

Jeannie put an arm across Marcus' shoulders. "I always hate it when your father has to go on business trips. I miss him like crazy."

"You know what they say," Marcus said as he leaned close to Jeannie and gave her a peck on the lips. "Absence makes the heart grow fonder."

Elle looked away in slight embarrassment, just as

Logan called out for help in the other room. She started to get up from her chair, but Jeannie stood first.

"You sit and relax," she said. "I got this."

"I'm happy for you," Marcus said when she left the room.

"Thanks," said Elle. "Where did that come from?"

"It just feels like it's been too long since you've been this animated. You have a glow about you, and it suits you."

"Well, thank you. I'm happy."

"I'm glad," he said. "Raiden's a great guy. And it's obvious he cares about Logan as well." He gave a nod towards the other room. "And Logan obviously thinks the world of him."

She frowned. "I have to admit that worries me though. What happens if things don't...you know."

"Don't worry about it right now, Elle," he said, shaking his head. "Just be happy."

"I'll do my best," she said, nodding. "Can I help you with dishes?"

"Of course," he said and they both stood.

"Has Raiden said anything about this case he's been working on?" Marcus asked as he and Elle cleared the table. "The pro bono one?"

"I know he does a lot of pro bono work," she

said, stacking all the plates on her arm while Marcus gathered the silverware. "But he hasn't mentioned anything specific to me."

"It's this kid, a juvenile case." Marcus shook his head in concern. "He's gotten himself into some real trouble. Not sure why Raiden doesn't just hand it off to the public defender."

"Maybe he sees something you don't." She followed her father into the kitchen.

"I don't know," he said. "I'm sure Raiden's heart is in the right place. Personally, I think he's wasting his time with this one. I'm sure it looks good on a resume at the end of the day, though."

"I highly doubt that's why he's helping him, Dad," she said, dropping the plates into the sink with a clatter.

Marcus turned on the tap and started rinsing them.

"Why else would he take on a lost cause like this one then?" he asked, handing a rinsed dish to Elle.

"Perhaps he's genuinely trying to help the kid," she said as she loaded it into the dishwasher.

"The kid's a mess. Even if Raiden does manage to keep him out of juvi this time, he's only prolonging the inevitable."

Elle stood up straight and faced her father. "You don't really feel that way, do you Dad?" she asked.

"Obviously I can't go into specifics, but I can tell a kid like that isn't going to amount to much."

Elle narrowed her eyes as her father tried to hand her another dish, but she didn't take it. "How can you say that? How can you know that Raiden won't make a difference in this kid's life? Even if it *is* a long shot, isn't it worth a try?"

Marcus set down the dish he had been trying to hand to her. "Now, honey. *You* don't really feel that way, do you? Give me one example. One success story." He folded his arms across his chest. "Support your argument."

Elle's heart pounded against her chest. She took a deep breath.

"I can't," she said.

"I rest my case," said Marcus, who turned back to the sink, and Elle felt her blood start to boil. She's always hated it when he said those words.

"I didn't say I don't know any," she said defiantly. "I just can't share it with you. I promised not to say anything."

"Why would you promise not to say anything?" he asked with a frown. "Why wouldn't you want other people to know about something potentially inspirational?"

Elle looked at her dad without answering his questions. She'd already said too much. How could she let the conversation go down this route? She should have just let it go. But it was frustrating to think that Marcus could be so narrow-minded.

"What going on, Elle? Is it someone I know?"

She bit her lip and Marcus' eyebrows went up.

"Oh. It's Raiden, isn't it? Is that why this case means so much to him?"

"I promised not to say anything," she repeated, much quieter this time.

"You're saying Raiden had his own troubles. When? What was it? Drugs, theft?"

Elle felt a little sick to her stomach.

"It was when he was a teenager. And it doesn't matter now. He obviously put himself on a better track. Look at everything he's accomplished now."

Now it was Marcus' turn to go silent, and the knot in her gut only tightened.

"He only recently told me and didn't want you to know because he thought you would hold it against him, that you might fire him over his past."

"I see," Marcus said, looking away.

"I told him that was ridiculous, that you aren't that petty. Right, Dad?"

But he wouldn't meet her eye.

"Right, Dad?" she asked more forcefully.

"Sure," he said. But Elle didn't believe him for a second. And now she was going to have to explain everything to Raiden.

"It's getting late," she said. "I should get Logan home."

"Of course," said Marcus.

She rounded up Logan and Marcus walked her to the door.

"Please don't hold this against Raiden," she pleaded. "Please."

"I just need to think about it," he said.

"That doesn't sound reassuring," she said.

"Everything will be fine," he said with a forced smile. "Don't worry about it."

But worrying was all Elle could do on the drive home, and as soon as Logan was tucked in for the night, she called Raiden's cell even though he wasn't due to land for several more hours.

"Raiden," she said after the beep. "I know you won't get this for a while, but I had to tell you right away before I chicken out." She took a deep breath and slowly exhaled. "I don't how to say this, but I accidentally told my dad more than I should have. He started talking about this case of yours and, well, it didn't go as well as I had hoped, but I'm sure it will be fine. It's just a shock to him. He can be a little conservative at times, but it will be fine, I'm sure of it." She hoped. "Call me when you can tomorrow. I love you."

She hung up and sank into the couch. What were they going to do if it wasn't okay?

The plane touched down in Seattle just after nine and Raiden rubbed the sleep from his eyes as he powered up the phone. As tired as he was, seeing the voicemail alert from Elle put a smile on his face. God, he couldn't wait to see her this afternoon. He might just have to stop by her office before he went home to crash.

But the smile disappeared as he listened to the message. He waited until he was off the plane to call her, but it started ringing before he had a chance to dial. His heart sank when Marcus' name popped up.

"Hello," he said hesitantly.

"Raiden, I take it you've landed already." Marcus' tone sounded pleasant enough.

"Walking through the airport to customs right now. What can I do for you?"

"I know you're probably exhausted, jet lag and all, but I was hoping you could stop in before heading home."

Raiden sighed. "Does this have anything to do with what you and Elle talked about last night?"

"Ah, so you've spoken with her already."

"There was a message from her when I landed."

"Why don't you just come in and we can talk?"

"Of course, sir."

"Good," said Marcus. "I'll see you soon then."

Raiden hung up the phone and immediately pulled up Elle's number. His heart pounded as it rang. Everything he had worked so hard for might come crashing down around him any minute now.

"You're home!" she said.

"What exactly did you tell your father?" he asked.

"I'm so sorry, I swear I didn't mean to."

"What did you tell him?" he repeated.

"Nothing specific. I told him you were a teenager and that none of it even—"

"He's just called me into his office," Raiden said. "He says he wants to talk."

"I'll call him right now," she said. "I'll talk some sense into him."

Raiden stopped walking and closed his eyes for a second. "Please don't do that, Elle."

"But I can fix this." The pleading in her voice made his heart ache.

"Just please don't. I don't need you making this any worse."

"Raiden…."

"I'll call you later." He ended the call before she could say anything else.

"Raiden…please," Elle said. But there was no sound on the other end, and she realized that Raiden had hung up. She laid her head on the desk and fought the urge to cry. Why couldn't she have just kept her big mouth shut?

Nine

Feeling like a zombie, Raiden stepped off the elevator and was immediately greeted by Cassie, who happened to be walking by.

"Raiden!" she said with more pep than he felt prepared to deal with at the moment. "I thought you were taking the day off to recover. You must be exhausted!"

He mustered a smile. "I just needed to talk to Marcus before I went home to crash."

"I think he's in his office now."

"Thanks, Cassie."

Marcus was seated at his desk, reading a file, but he looked up as soon as Raiden walked in.

"Close the door, please," he said.

Raiden did as he asked and sat down in one of the chairs facing him.

"So exactly what kind of trouble were you in?" Marcus asked, not wasting any time.

"I—I was part of a gang, sir," he said and watched Marcus blanch.

"What kind of gang are we talking about?" Marcus asked in shock. "Was this just neighborhood kids going around stirring up trouble? Or something more serious?"

"More serious," Raiden said.

"I see." Marcus frowned. "And were you ever involved in any illegal activities?"

Raiden nodded.

"Were you ever arrested?"

Raiden nodded again.

"How do I not know any of this?" There was no mistaking the anger in Marcus' voice. "How did this not show up in your background check? Hell, how did you ever pass the bar?"

Raiden could feel the heat rising in his chest and tried to imagine how he might feel if he were in Marcus' place. Because it was hard not to take Marcus' distrust personally.

"Because it was all expunged on my eighteenth birthday."

Raiden proceeded to tell him the same story he

had told Elle, and Marcus listened quietly, patiently. But the anger and distrust never left his face.

"You've put me in an awkward position," Marcus said when Raiden had finished.

"I don't understand how, sir," Raiden said, trying as hard as possible to keep his voice even. "I never lied about anything, and I don't have a criminal record."

"But what if clients find out that I have a former gang member working in my office?"

"No one would find out unless you or Elle decided to say something. The only reason I even said anything to her was because we ran into some old associates at a club the other night. Even then, she didn't know who or what they were."

"You exposed Elle to these people?" Marcus asked, furrowing his brow, and Raiden realized he probably should have left that part out.

"Not on purpose, of course. We were at a concert, and they happened to be in town for a wedding. I hadn't spoken to any of them since I left California."

Marcus steepled his fingers under his chin, and Raiden waited for him to speak.

"I think," he finally said, putting his hands down, "that it might be best if you don't take on any more clients for the time being."

"Are you serious?" Raiden asked. "You're firing me?"

"It's just temporary," said Marcus. "I need time to figure out how this is going to impact the firm. We'll tell people that your workload was becoming too much."

"I knew it," Raiden said, shaking his head. He stood up and made for the door.

"And one more thing," Marcus said, and Raiden reluctantly turned around. "I want you to stop seeing Elle."

It was like a punch to the gut, but Raiden shouldn't have been surprised.

"I don't feel comfortable with my daughter and grandson getting caught up in this."

"They're not in any danger," said Raiden. "I would never—"

"You just said that you ran into some old friends recently," Marcus cut in. "Who's to say it won't happen again? Or that they don't hold a grudge? No, you'll leave Elle and Logan alone. And you'll tell her it was your decision."

Raiden's hands balled into fists at his sides, and he jammed them into his pockets, fighting the urge to punch something.

"You're asking me to lie to your daughter," he said through clenched teeth. "You're asking me to abandon her."

"I'm asking you to protect her. If you really care about her…."

"I should go," he said, and Marcus nodded.

Raiden walked into his apartment to find Elle sitting on the sofa. She jumped up as he closed the door behind him.

"What did he say?" she asked, wringing her hands.

He said nothing as he dropped his keys in the dish and rolled his carry-on to the bedroom.

"Talk to me, Raiden."

"He said I shouldn't take on any more clients until he figures out what to do with me." Raiden walked over to the kitchen and pulled a bottle of scotch from a cabinet.

"I'm so sorry," she said, coming over to stand next to him as he poured a glass. "I never imagined." She placed a hand on his arm and he sighed.

"I know."

"I'll talk to him," she said. "I'll make him see how stupid he's being."

Raiden placed a hand over hers and thought about Marcus' final words back at the office.

"I think you've done enough," he said, swallowing hard as he turned to face her.

"What do you mean?" she asked.

"I mean that the damage is done. To my career and," he hesitated, "and to us."

Elle yanked her hand away as if she'd been stung.

"You can't mean that," she said.

He just stared at her, not saying anything. Her chin was starting to tremble, and he wanted to say the words that would make it stop. But maybe Marcus was right. Maybe he was the wrong man for Elle to be around.

"Please, Raiden," she begged, her eyes glistening. "Please don't do this. You promised me." Her last words were barely audible.

He pressed his forehead to hers, and she shocked him by grabbing his face and kissing him. God, he had missed her these last couple days. Yes, he was mad that she had said something to Marcus, but he didn't want to say goodbye. And he sure as hell didn't want to break her heart like this.

"You should go," he said, pushing her away.

Tears were welling in her eyes and she was doing her best to blink them away. He was just about to pull her back into him and say screw it when she turned on her heel, grabbed her purse, and walked out the door.

Raiden turned back to his glass of scotch and

pressed his palms against the counter. What a fool he'd been to think that someone like him could ever have it all. He stood up, drained the tumbler, and poured another glass.

Anger, guilt, and hurt took turns sweeping through Elle as she walked back to her office. She'd hoped the jaunt would help her calm down, but she felt no better by the time she arrived at her desk. She stood up and started packing up her stuff. She didn't care what Raiden said—Elle had to talk to her dad, even if it wouldn't fix anything.

"Sienna," she said, stopping by the front desk on her way out, "something's come up and I need to head out. Call me if you need anything."

Sienna nodded. "Is everything all right?"

"It's fine. Or it will be, I hope. I don't know." Elle walked out the door before Sienna could ask any more questions, or worse yet, before she started crying.

Cassie greeted Elle with a big warm smile that Elle just couldn't match.

"Is my dad in?" she asked.

"Yes, but he's stepping into a meeting any minute now."

Elle headed for his office without another word.

"How could you?" she asked as she walked in and shut the door behind her. Marcus looked up with a frown.

"I don't have time to talk about this, Elle."

"He broke up with me."

"It's probably for the best," Marcus said curtly as he stood and made for the door, but Elle held her ground. "Excuse me, please."

"What the hell is that supposed to mean?"

He sighed. "I didn't want to see you get hurt again."

"Didn't want…. Wait, did you put him up to this?"

"I was thinking of you and Logan. The last thing you need is another Jason in your life."

"Raiden is *nothing* like Jason. And you're the one who encouraged me to give Raiden a chance."

"If I'd know what Raiden really was," said Marcus, "I never would have."

"What he really is?" Elle narrowed her eyes at her father. "What exactly is it that you think Raiden is, Dad?"

Marcus waved a hand in the air. "You know what I mean."

"No," she said, planting her hands on her hips, "I don't."

"He's a thug, Elle." Her jaw dropped. "That's

what I'm trying to say. And I don't know why I didn't see it before."

"Unbelievable."

"You and Logan don't need someone like that in your lives." He started rubbing his temple as he looked around. "I just need to figure out how to let him go without all of this getting out."

"You're right. Raiden has a shady past, one that he's not proud of. But he's worked his ass off to prove that's not who he really is. Because what he is is generous, compassionate, and caring. I think you're the one Logan and I don't need in our lives. I won't raise Logan with a bigot for a grandfather influencing him."

Marcus scowled at her. "Don't you think that's a bit extreme?" he said in the same tone he used when sending her to her room as a teenager. But this time she was in the right. It was her father who was being unreasonable.

"No," she said, and there was a knock at the door. Before she could say anything else, Cassie poked her head into the room.

"Marcus," she said. "They're all waiting for you."

"We'll talk about this later," Marcus said as Elle let him slip past.

"Not unless you're telling me you've had a

change of heart," she said quietly.

He gave her a look before turning and heading down the hall.

"Is everything okay?" Cassie asked, looking bewildered.

"No, it's not." And Elle walked out without any further explanation.

Elle's hand shook as she tried to put her key in the ignition. Had she really just stood up to her father? She took a deep breath before putting the car in reverse. She was hanging by a thread right now and just needed to make it home before she fell apart.

The house was quiet when Elle walked in, and she sent a text asking Missy to bring Logan home when she picked him up. That gave Elle two hours to pull herself together. She headed upstairs to her bed, where she curled into a ball and waited for the tears to come. But she was too numb to cry. She couldn't decide who she was angrier with—her father for being so two-faced, Raiden for listening to her father, or herself for letting Raiden's secret slip. He'd warned her, hadn't he? It bothered her that Raiden had known her father better than she had. How naive she had been.

The doorbell rang, but Elle just continued to lie

there. She heard the door opening and she sat up in fear.

"Elle?"

She jumped up at the sound of Raiden's voice. There was a creaking on the steps, and she walked out to find him halfway up the stairs.

"Elle," he said again, stopping.

She looked at him, not saying anything. There was only one reason he would have come to the house, but she was scared to hope.

He walked up a couple more steps until his face was level with hers.

"I'm sorry," he said. "I don't know what I was thinking."

"I know my father told you to do it," she said.

"I shouldn't have listened," he said, shaking his head.

"I'm so sorry, this is all my fault." She felt the tears finally spilling over, and Raiden moved closer to wrap his arms around her.

"No, this isn't."

"If I'd just kept my mouth shut," she mumbled into his solid chest. "You were right. I wanted to think the best of my father, but you were right."

"This isn't on you," he said, rubbing her back. "It's all me. I should've known that it would all come out eventually. I shouldn't have tried so hard to hide it."

She pulled away and wiped her face.

"I told him to stay away from Logan and me if this was how he really felt."

"Why would you do that?" Raiden asked with a frown. "He's your father."

"He's not the great man I always imagined him to be."

"We all have our prejudices, Elle. He thinks he's protecting you and his business."

"Are you saying you agree with him?" she asked incredulously.

"Of course not. But he's your father, the man who raised you when your mother walked out. You can't cut him out of your life because of me."

"I don't want to choose, but if I have to, then I choose you."

"Oh, Elle," he said and kissed her.

She welcomed his lips on hers—how many days had it been? Her hands instinctively moved up to his head and pulled her deeper into him.

"God, I've missed you," he said, and his mouth worked its way down her neck.

"What are you going to do?" she asked, still worried about the whole situation. "For work, I mean. If you're let go."

"I'll figure something out." He stood up and gave

her a devilish grin that made her heart pound faster. "Besides, it's not really where my mind is at right now."

Raiden woke the next morning to find Elle fully dressed.

"Good morning," she said, sitting on the bed next to him. "How do you feel?"

"Jet-lagged," he said, rubbing his eyes.

"I figured as much. There's nothing in the house for breakfast, so I was going to run out and grab bagels. Do you want me to bring Logan along?"

"Nah, it's fine. I can hang with him."

"Are you sure? You can sleep longer if I take him with me."

Raiden sat up. "It's fine. I might sleep the whole day away if you let me."

"I'll be back soon, then," she said, kissing his cheek.

He climbed out of bed wearing the lounge pants he had started keeping at Elle's and headed downstairs. Logan was sitting at the coffee table coloring.

"Morning, Raiden," he said with a big grin on his face

"Good morning," Raiden said, tousling Logan's auburn hair. "What are you drawing there?"

"It's you and me and mommy," he said, proudly holding up what he had done so far. "And we're at the park."

"Wow." Raiden took it from him. "That's…really awesome." He never thought that appearing in a kid's drawing could mean so much to him. "Good job, Logan," he said, handing it back.

Logan focused on his masterpiece again and Raiden wandered into the kitchen, where he found half a pot of coffee still left. He poured himself a cup and headed back into the other room, sitting on the couch.

"Mind if I turn on some news?" he asked, grabbing the remote as Logan shook his head.

But there was a knock at the door before he had a chance to hit the power button. Raiden peeked through the curtain behind him and recognized Marcus' car out front.

"Crap," he muttered just quiet enough so that Logan couldn't hear.

Setting his cup on the table, he made his way to the door. He paused, wondering if he should just ignore it, since Marcus was clearly here to see Elle, who wasn't home yet. But then he remembered that his car was also parked out front and was sure Marcus had seen it. With a tightness in his chest, he reluctantly opened the door.

"Raiden," Marcus said, frowning. "I was expecting Elle."

"She just stepped out for bagels but should be back soon."

"I see."

"Would you like to come in and wait for her?" Raiden asked.

"Yes. Please."

"Papa!" Logan exclaimed as soon as he saw him. He jumped up and raced into his grandfather's welcoming arms.

"How's my Logan?" Marcus asked.

"Good."

Marcus looked at Raiden, who was feeling more uncomfortable by the second. "I take it you spent the night here."

Raiden could only nod as he crossed his arms over his bare chest.

"Look what I drew!" Logan said, jumping from Marcus' arms and grabbing his picture from the table.

Marcus kneeled down to look at it. "I take it this is you and mommy." Logan nodded. "And who is this?" he asked pointing at the third caricature. "Is this me?"

"No, silly," Logan laughed. "It's Raiden."

Marcus smiled, but Raiden had no doubt that it

was forced.

"If you want," Raiden said, taking a step toward the stairs, "I could leave you and Logan here to wait for Elle."

"No need," said Marcus. "And I'm sure Elle wouldn't be too happy about that."

"Probably not."

Raiden looked at Logan, who had gone back to the table and grabbed a fresh sheet to make a new drawing. One that included his grandfather this time, perhaps.

"I know that she came to see you yesterday after I left," he told Marcus. "I hope you know I had no idea. I never wanted to come between you two."

"I know," said Marcus. "Let's go in the kitchen and talk."

Raiden grabbed his coffee mug as they moved though the living room.

"We'll just be in the other room if you need anything. Okay, little man?"

"Okay," said Logan.

"Can I get you a cup of coffee?" Raiden asked, leaning against the counter as Marcus sank into one of the chairs at the kitchen table.

"I'm good, thank you." Marcus cleared his throat. "After Elle told me she didn't want me around anymore, I was hurt just as much as I was angry."

Raiden wasn't sure how to respond, so he remained quiet and waited for Marcus to continue.

"By the time I got home last night, I found myself wondering what kind of daughter I had raised that would be so rash. But the more I thought about everything she said, the more I began to think that she may have been right. About me, that is." He looked up at Raiden with a weak smile. "Turns out I did an even more amazing job raising her than I would have thought possible. Someone who is clearly far more open-minded than I am and is able to see the good in people."

"She's one of the most amazing people I know," said Raiden, looking him right in the eye. "And I would never hurt her if I can help it."

"I'm sorry for over-reacting."

"Does that mean I still have a job?" Raiden asked, not bothering to beat around the bush.

"Yes."

"And it's not going to bother you that I will continue to see Elle so long as she'll have me?"

Marcus nodded.

"Then apology accepted," said Raiden.

"That being said, however, it still makes me uncomfortable that you ran into those former…associates."

"It didn't sit well with me either, so I made some

calls. The gang is all but dissolved now. Most of the members are currently in jail, including the leader, who's doing life. The days for retaliation are long gone. And if anyone was going to approach me, they would have done it by now."

"I see," said Marcus.

"Doesn't mean I'm not always watching my back though," Raiden said, and he took a sip of coffee.

The front door could be heard opening, and seconds later Elle walked into the kitchen with a bag, looking worried.

"Dad, what are you doing here?"

"It's fine," Raiden said, taking the bag from her.

"Is it?" she asked, looking from him to her father.

"As much as I hate to admit it," Marcus said, standing, "you were right about me being pig-headed."

"And?"

"And what?" her father replied.

"And what about Raiden's job?" she asked.

"I told you it's fine," said Raiden.

"There is one thing though," Marcus said.

"I knew it," Elle said, narrowing her eyes at him, and Raiden placed a calming hand on her back.

"I would still appreciate it if none of this got out to anyone else at the office or any of our clients."

"Seriously?" Elle snapped.

"He's right," Raiden told her. "We can't know who will take this the wrong way or try to use it against us."

Marcus nodded.

"And it's not exactly something I want to be common knowledge anyway," said Raiden.

"You're probably right," said Elle.

"So we're all on the same page then?" Marcus asked and everyone nodded. "In that case," he continued, "does that mean I can take my grandson to breakfast?"

"Of course," Elle said.

"Logan," Marcus called out as he walked back into the living room. "Would you like to go get pancakes with me?"

Logan's whoop of excitement rang through the whole house.

"I'll have him back by lunch," Marcus called out, and they headed out the front door.

"Do you know what this means?" Elle asked as she turned and wrapped her arms around Raiden's neck.

"That after the most tense twenty-four hours," he said, wrapping his arms around her waist, "everything is right with the world again."

"That too," she said with a playful smile. "But it also means we have an empty house for the next couple hours."

"Well, I guess we'd better not waste it."

"Mommy, mommy!" Logan came barreling into the kitchen where Elle was putting in the last pan of chocolate chip cookies. "Can we go now?" he asked.

"Oh, Sweetie," she said. "We aren't leaving for at least another hour. We still have to wait for Raiden to get back with all the stuff."

"But that's going to take forever," he sighed, plopping onto one of the dining chairs. "I wanna go fishing now."

"I know, Logan." She wiped her hands and crouched down to look him in the eye. "Why don't you run upstairs and choose one special stuffed animal to bring with you, okay?"

"Okay." He took off running, and Elle knew she had just bought herself a good fifteen minutes while he tried to decide which one was his favorite today.

For the last two weeks, fishing had been all Logan could talk about. This weekend Raiden was taking them camping—a first for both her and Logan—and Raiden had promised to teach Logan how to fish. Elle was terrified, but Raiden had promised her it would be great. And that there would be bathrooms with running water and showers. He had all the gear in storage, which he went to collect after picking up the SUV rental, and she was in charge of the food.

Now she was standing next to the bins on the kitchen table, checking off the contents against the list Raiden had made for her. She didn't know the first thing you were supposed to eat while "roughing it."

The oven timer went off, and Elle slipped on some mitts just as the doorbell rang.

Logan's footsteps thundered down the stairs. "Yay! Raiden's here, now we can go fishing!"

Elle sighed. She decided she would let Raiden explain this time why they couldn't leave just yet.

"She's in here," she heard Logan say, and then footsteps coming down the hall. She looked up with a big grin that disappeared when saw that it wasn't Raiden behind Logan.

"Hello, Elle," said Jason.

Ten

"Who's ready to go fishing?" Raiden called out as he walked through Elle's front door. Logan jumped up and ran to him, but it was the presence of another man sitting on the floor next to a pile of Legos that caught him off guard. Raiden realized in that moment that apart from Elle's steel-colored eyes, Logan was the spitting image of his father.

"Who is this?" said Jason, and Raiden wanted to deck him. What right did this man have to question Elle's guest?

Elle, who had jumped off the couch at Raiden's arrival, said, "This is Raiden." She signaled Raiden towards the kitchen. "We need to talk."

Raiden could feel the man's gaze on him as he

walked across the living room, but Raiden kept his chin held high. He was the one who belonged here, not Jason.

"Who is Raiden?" he heard Jason ask Logan as he sat back down on the floor.

"He's our friend," answered Logan. "He's going to teach me how to fish."

"What is he doing here?" Raiden asked Elle when they got to the kitchen.

"He received the papers and flew out. I didn't know he was coming, he just showed up a little bit ago."

"Did he sign them?"

She shook her head.

"Is he going to?"

"I don't know. We haven't really talked yet. He's been playing with Logan this whole time."

"There's action you can take if he won't sign them; he hasn't even been in the state for the last two years. You have a really strong case." But then Raiden saw the look on her face. "You do still want to divorce him, don't you?"

"I don't know," she said, tears welling in the corner of her eyes. "This is so confusing. I never expected him to come back. Shouldn't I at least hear him out?"

Raiden shook his head at her. "You can't let him

do this to you. It's not fair to you guys. He can't expect you to put your life on hold and then drop everything when he decides to play house again."

"But he's Logan's father." She shook her head slightly. "He's…he's my husband."

"Only on paper. A real father or husband would never do that to his family. *I* would never do that to you."

"You can't make that promise, no one can. Because I'm pretty sure Jason said the same thing on our wedding day."

He took her by the shoulders and looked her straight in the face. "I'm telling you, Elle, I would never do that. I'm not Jason. I love you." Her breath hitched at his words. "You and Logan."

He continued to stare into her eyes and he felt his words sinking in to her, but then Logan ran in and she took a step back to wipe her face.

"Raiden, I'm ready to go fishing! When are we going?"

Raiden kneeled down before Logan, ignoring Jason leaning against the wall behind him.

"It looks like we're going to have to wait to go fishing, little man."

"But you promised!"

"I know, but I didn't know your dad would be showing up, and I think you should spend some time with him. I hear it's been a long time since you've seen him," Raiden said, giving Jason a look.

"Okay, but you promise we'll go later?"

"Of course. You just call me when you're ready. Deal?"

"Deal." Logan gave him a big hug, and Raiden's heart ached. As he held Logan in a big bear hug, he was mentally yelling, "Pick me, Elle, pick me. I'm not ready to lose you guys." But he said nothing as he released Logan, stood up, and gave Elle a nod before heading back out.

Elle stood in the kitchen and watched Raiden disappear, his shoulders slumped, and it broke her heart. The front door banged shut and Jason finally spoke.

"Who is Raiden?" he asked.

"I told you," said Logan, "he's our friend."

Jason ignored Logan as he stared at Elle, waiting for the real explanation.

"Logan, sweetie," she said, looking back at her husband, who she still couldn't believe was standing in her house for the first time in two years, "why don't you go back in the other room and play with your Legos some more."

He didn't need to be asked twice, and when she heard the clacking of plastic bricks, she asked Jason her own question.

"What are you doing here?"

"I've come to make things right," he said.

She frowned. "Why now? After all this time, why did you finally come back?"

He took a step toward her and rested a hand on the back of a dining chair.

"Because you sent me divorce papers. What else was I supposed to do?"

"You were supposed to sign them and send them back," she said, rubbing her forehead. "They were not an invitation to come back here. And I sent those papers two months ago, what the hell took you so long?"

"I've been traveling," he said, and she shook her head in disbelief. "It took a while for them to get to me." He stepped even closer to her and placed a warm hand on her cheek. "But I flew out as soon as I saw them. I realized it was time to come home."

She carefully removed his hand from her face. "You're too late," she whispered.

"Why?" He frowned. "Is it because of this Raiden guy? Are you two getting married? Is that why you took so long to file?"

"No," she said. "I mean, yes, he's the reason I finally filed, but not because we're getting married. He helped me realize that I should have filed the day you walked out."

"Please, Elle. I know I messed up. But let me make it up to you and Logan."

Elle looked past Jason toward the living room, where she could hear Logan still playing. It should be so easy to say no to Jason, to say that she was in love with Raiden. But what about Logan? What was best for him?

"I need to think about it," she found herself saying.

"Thank you," he said and kissed her on the cheek. He turned around and went into the other room to join their son.

Elle sat down at the table and buried her head in her hands. It was all just so confusing.

After returning the truck to the rental place, Raiden walked into his apartment and immediately went to the fridge to grab a beer. He popped the top and moved to the couch, where he sank into it. Without taking a drink, he set the bottle on the coffee table and found himself wondering what was going on at Elle and Logan's house. Were she and Jason talking? Was Jason telling Elle everything she had been waiting to hear? And then he wondered where Jason was going to sleep tonight, and the thought made him sick to his stomach. Surely she wasn't going to share her bed with Jason. He tried to remind himself that Elle loved him. Whatever confusion she might be feeling right now, it was Raiden that she loved. Wasn't it?

Raiden knew he couldn't just sit here all day hoping for the best, so he left the untouched beer on the table and went to change into workout clothes. Time to burn some nervous energy off at the gym.

Elle leaned against the archway dividing the living room from the kitchen, watching Jason and Logan play the game that Raiden had brought over not so long ago. Logan looked as happy as could be, but the whole scene irritated her. Once upon a time she would have said this was how it should have been, but not anymore. Jason had shown his true colors. She now realized it was Raiden who should be here in this house with them, not Jason.

"Time for bed, Logan," she said, pushing off the wall.

"Aw, Mom," he groaned. "But we're having fun!"

"Yeah, Mom," said Jason with a grin. "Don't be such a party pooper."

"I was being nice by letting him stay up an hour past bedtime," she said as she turned off the television in the middle of their game.

"Is she always this mean?" Jason asked Logan in jest. But Logan just looked at him in confusion.

"Mommy's not mean," he said, and Elle could have done a cartwheel.

"Of course not," said Jason, giving her an apologetic smile. "I bet she's a pretty awesome mom."

Elle shook her head.

"She is awesome!" Logan said as he let Elle pick him up.

"Thanks, Sweetie," she said, giving him a genuine smile. "I think you're pretty awesome too."

His whole face lit up.

"Now say goodnight to Daddy," she told him.

"Goodnight Daddy," he said obediently.

"Goodnight Logan," said Jason. "See you in the morning."

Elle helped Logan get into pajamas and brush his teeth before tucking him into bed. His sleepy head wouldn't be awake for long.

"Is Daddy staying?" he asked between yawns.

"He's staying the night," she said, although she suspected that wasn't exactly what he was asking.

"But for how long? Is he going to live with us?"

Elle sighed. "I don't know how long for. But I don't think he's going to live with us."

"Why not?" he asked.

"Well…." She wasn't quite sure how to explain it to a four-year-old. The simplest answer she knew was because she'd rather Raiden was living with them. But she didn't want to make things complicated for Logan.

"We'll just have to see what happens," was the answer she finally settled for. To be honest, she had no idea what Jason was planning. It was time to go downstairs and find out.

"You get some sleep," she said, kissing Logan's forehead. "And I will see you in the morning."

"Okay," he said. "I love you Mommy."

"I love you too. Forever and ever."

"Forever and ever," he repeated with a sleepy smile.

When Logan was finally asleep, Elle grabbed an extra pillow and blanket and headed downstairs, where she left them on the couch, then moved into the kitchen where Jason was at the kitchen table with an open bottle of her favorite Cabernet Franc and two glasses already poured.

She wanted to protest—what right did he have—but the truth was a glass of wine was exactly what she needed.

"Thanks," she mumbled as she sat down across from him and took a sip.

"He's gotten so big," Jason said, rolling the stem of his glass between his thumb and forefinger. "I mean, he's talking in full sentences and everything."

As he fiddled with the wine glass, Elle noticed for the first time that Jason was still wearing his wedding ring. She glanced down at her own hand where even the tan line of her ring had long faded.

"Did you ever miss us?" she asked, almost choking on the words.

Jason looked up at her with wide eyes. "Of course I did. All the time."

"But not enough to come home?"

"I was a coward."

"That's not a very good reason," she said.

"I know. But it's the truth. I panicked and ran away. And the longer I stayed away, the harder it was to reach out to you. But when I saw the papers, it was now or never."

She looked down at her glass before taking a big swig.

"I love you, Elle," he said, and she looked back up at him.

"Then why did you leave us in the first place?"

"I panicked. I felt like I was in way over my head, and I panicked. I'm sorry."

"I could understand taking a couple days," she said, trying to keep her voice as calm as possible.

"Maybe even a week or so. But two goddamn years!"

"Shh," said Jason. "You might wake Logan."

"Logan is too heavy a sleeper. If you had been around, you would know that."

Jason leaned back in the chair, his mouth in a tight line, but said nothing.

"You have been gone for half of your son's life," she said, lowering her voice anyway. "He doesn't have a single memory of you other than pictures. And he's already asking if you'll go away again." She watched the pained expression on Jason's face at these words and leaned across the table towards him. "Do you honestly think that I haven't had moments of panic? I panic every time I lose sight of him at the park or the grocery store. I panicked when I had to rush him to the doctor with a hundred and two degree fever. I panic when I think that if something were to happen to me he wouldn't have anyone else. All parents panic. It's called being a grown-up."

"I know there's no excuse for what I did to you two. But I've changed. Please let me prove it to you," he pleaded.

Elle took another drink, trying to think of what to do.

"Are you and this Raiden guy serious?" he asked.

Another sip. "Yes."

"So you're sleeping together?"

She looked into his hazel eyes. "Can you honestly say you haven't slept with anyone else since you left me?"

"No," he said, staring right back. "I haven't."

"Well your loss then," she said, and her hands shook as she refilled her glass. This whole time she had imagined him out gallivanting, enjoying his "single" life. Assuming he was telling the truth, did this change anything?

She picked up the wine glass and stood. "I'm going to bed," she said. "I left you a pillow and blanket on the couch."

He gave a somber nod, no longer looking at her. She started to walk out of the room, but then she stopped and turned around.

"Not that it's really any of your business," she said, and Jason looked up at her, "but Raiden is the only person I've been with since you. Not even so much as a date before him. Because it took me that long to realize I shouldn't be putting my life on pause for someone who didn't want to be around."

"Are you happy?" he asked, surprising her with the unexpected response.

"Yes, I am," she said with confidence.

"Happier than you were with me?"

Her confidence faltered. "That's not a fair question."

"Are you?" he asked again.

"I'm going to bed." And she left with his question still echoing in her ears.

Elle walked into the kitchen the next morning to find Logan at the table with a syrup-covered face and Jason at the stove.

"Look, Mommy," Logan said when she sat down next to him. "Daddy made Mickey Mouse pancakes."

Jason turned around to flash her a smile, but she couldn't return it. So this is what it could have been like had he not walked out the door that day. Or at the very least came back a hell of a lot sooner.

"For m'lady," Jason said as he set a plate of hotcakes on the table in front of her.

"I'm not very hungry," she said.

"But they're really yummy, Mommy."

She smiled at Logan. "Will you share this one with me then?"

He nodded with enthusiasm.

Jason sat down and made silly faces at Logan while they ate. If Jason made him laugh as easily as Raiden did, would Logan be quick to forget about Raiden? Elle knew that would break Raiden's heart just as much as hers did at the thought.

When Logan had finished his last bite, Elle took the dirty plates to the sink.

"Go upstairs, Sweetie, and get dressed."

"Okay." He slid out of his chair and headed out the kitchen.

"And don't forget to wash your face first," she called after him.

"I know I said it already," Jason said, watching him go, "but God, that kid has gotten big."

Elle just sighed as she rinsed the breakfast dishes piled in the sink.

"Did you guys have anything planned for today?" he asked.

"We were supposed to be camping right now."

"I still can't believe you were going to camp. That would have been humorous."

She shut the water off and turned around. "What is it going to take to get you to sign the papers?"

The office was quiet when Raiden stepped off the elevator. He thought he heard someone in the break room, but he was in no mood for talking, so he bee-lined it to his office.

Making notes on a recent deposition was not how he really wanted to spend a Saturday morning, but anything beat sitting at home waiting for Elle to call.

Or worrying about what she might call to say.

"Raiden?"

He looked up to see Marcus standing in his doorway.

"What are you doing here?" he asked. "Aren't you supposed to be camping with Elle and Logan?"

"I take it Elle hasn't talked to you."

"No. Why? Did something happen to Logan?"

"They're fine, Marcus, it's just that….Well, I think you should talk to Elle."

"What's going on, Raiden?" he asked with a stern voice.

"Jason came back yesterday. Right before we were supposed to leave."

"What? Why? Did he sign the papers?"

"I don't know, sir. But you should really talk to your daughter."

If Raiden couldn't talk some sense into Elle, maybe her father would have better luck.

"Let's go for a walk," said Jason.

"A walk?" She was asking him for a divorce, and all he wanted was to go for a walk.

"Yeah," he said. "We could walk through the Arboretum across the street like we did when Logan was a baby."

Elle had made that walk so many times with

Logan that she had forgotten there was a time when Jason had made it with them.

"And we can talk," he added.

She wasn't entirely sure what there was left to talk about, but Elle decided it couldn't hurt.

"Fine. I'll get Logan ready."

They walked in silence to the expansive nature area near Elle's house with Logan between them.

"Are you sure you want a divorce?" Jason asked, and Elle wondered if he had spent as much of the night mulling things over as she had.

Her phone started ringing before she had a chance to answer and knew from the tone that it was her father. If he was calling her, then he must know she wasn't camping, which meant Raiden had said something. *Dammit.*

She sighed as she prepared to answer.

"Sorry," she said to Jason and pressed the phone to her ear. "Hello."

Her father wasted no time.

"Raiden told me that Jason came back."

"Yes," was all she said.

"Is he there now?"

"Yes." She avoided looking at Jason.

"I'm coming over," he said. "You shouldn't say anything without me there."

"No! We're not even home right now—"

"Where are you? Did he take you somewhere? You aren't leaving with him, are you?"

"No! We're just out for a walk. Let me call you back."

"You don't owe that bastard anything," said Marcus.

"I know. Let me call you back later."

There was silence on the other end.

"Please," she begged.

"All right," he said. "Just be careful. I love you."

"I love you too."

She hung up the phone and saw the daggers shooting from Jason's eyes.

"Was that Raiden?" he asked, and Elle shook her head.

"It was my dad."

"You called your dad?"

"No, Raiden must have said something." She saw the look of confusion on his face. "They, um, they work together."

Jason's eyebrows went up. "Oh. And what did Marcus have to say?"

She shook her head again. "He's just worried is all."

Jason shoved his hands in his pockets and looked straight ahead.

"Yes," she said, looking down at her feet.

"Yes what?" he asked, turning to face her, but she couldn't meet his gaze.

"Yes is the answer to your question. I'm sure I want a divorce."

"What if—" he paused, "what if we gave us a try again? Say a month?"

Elle stopped walking and focused on Logan up ahead, who was watching a bug climb a bench. How long had she waited for Jason to come home and say those words? Or at least something along those lines.

"I'm in love with Raiden," she said, turning to look Jason in the eye. "Completely and utterly in love."

"But what about us?" Jason asked. "What we had? We have a son together for crying out loud!"

"You're right, we did have something good. And when you walked out the door, you broke it. You shattered my heart into a million little pieces. And it's Raiden who has put those pieces back together, who showed me what it was like to be loved again."

"Please Elle…." She could see the tears forming in Jason's eyes. The only other time he had cried was at the birth of Logan. But it didn't change a thing. It didn't change what he did to them when they needed him most.

"If you had come back before I met him," she said, "before I had served you with divorce papers, I would have said yes in a heartbeat. And it would have been a mistake. Seeing how Raiden treats us and wants to take care of us, I now know what we would have been missing out on."

"How do you know he won't walk when the going gets tough either?" he asked.

She shook her head. "You're just saying that because you're desperate." She started to walk towards Logan.

"But what if?" He called after her.

Elle spun around. "Unlike you, Raiden is willing to fight for the things he loves, no matter how tough it is. But if he did, then he wouldn't deserve me either." She turned back to Logan. "C'mon Sweetie, I think we should head home now."

"So that's it," Jason said as he followed her and took one of Logan's hands. "You're denying me my son because you're in love with some other guy?"

Elle eyed Jason's grip on Logan's hand, but Logan didn't seem to mind.

"That's not what I'm saying," she told Jason. "Of course you can see your son. But you and I are through. We can work out a custody plan and then I expect you to sign the papers."

"I don't want a custody plan, I want us to be a family, the way it was supposed to be."

"That ship sailed a long time ago. Will you

please let go of Logan's hand?" she asked gently.

Jason looked down at Logan, who was starting to look uncomfortable in his grasp, and released it.

Elle could tell that Jason was fuming as they headed back to the house, but he didn't say anything. When they had to cross the busy intersection, Jason picked up Logan and carried him across the street in his arms.

"What the fuck…" she heard him say as they approached the house.

"Watch your language," she said, looking up to see her father and Raiden waiting in front of her house. Fuck was right.

"Here they come," said Marcus.

Raiden looked up from where he was sitting on the front step and saw Elle and Jason walking towards them, Logan perched in Jason's arm. They looked like…a family. Raiden's chest constricted.

Elle rushed ahead of Jason and Logan, and Raiden stood.

"What are you guys doing here?" she seethed.

"We came to talk some sense in to you," said Marcus.

She looked betrayed as she glanced at Raiden.

"It was his idea," he mumbled to her.

"What's going on?" Jason asked, setting Logan

on the grass.

"Are we going fishing now, Raiden?" Logan asked.

"Not yet, little man," Raiden said, tousling his hair.

"Logan," Elle said, getting eye level with him, "can you play out here with daddy for a little bit while I talk to Papa and Raiden?" Logan nodded and she looked up at Jason, who didn't look happy but nodded as well.

Raiden followed her and Marcus into the house.

"Seriously, what were you guys thinking coming here?" she asked the second Raiden closed the door behind him. He knew this hadn't been a good idea.

"We're worried about you," said Marcus. "I just wanted to make sure that Jason didn't try to take advantage of you."

"You honestly think I can't take care of myself?"

"Are you giving him another chance?" Raiden asked. It was the only reason he had agreed to come.

Elle looked at him, and he watched her expression soften. "No," she said. "I've told him that's not happening."

"And he's okay with it?" Marcus asked.

"No. But it doesn't matter." She continued to look at Raiden and he swallowed hard. He wasn't losing them after all. "Jason and I were done a long time ago, whatever delusions he may be holding on to."

"Have you told him specifically that you want a divorce?" Marcus asked.

Elle finally tore her eyes from Raiden. "Yes, just a little bit ago in the park. I told him we could work out a custody plan and then I expected him to sign the papers."

"Good," said Marcus. "Then we should ask him to vacate the property and to find a lawyer before contacting you again."

"Is that really necessary?" Elle asked, frowning.

"It's for the best," Raiden told her as he turned to open the door.

"Wait," she said, placing a hand on his arm to stop him. "Let me do the talking. There's no need to be confrontational about this."

Raiden nodded and the three of them filed out to the now empty yard.

"Logan!" Raiden called out.

"Where'd they go?" Marcus asked.

"Oh my God," she said, covering her mouth with her hands.

"What?" he asked, but he already knew.

She lowered her hands. "You don't think—" Her voice choked on the words.

"No," Raiden whispered, shaking his head.

"I'm calling the police," said Marcus.

"Hold on," Raiden yelled out. "Let's not jump to conclusions." He moved closer to Elle. "Do you honestly think Jason would kidnap Logan?"

"I don't know," she said. "I don't think so. Oh my God, what if he did?"

Raiden placed his hands on her shoulders and could feel her trembling. "I need you to think. Has he done anything to suggest he might have been planning it?"

"I—no. But then where the hell is my son?"

"Do you have his cell number?" Raiden asked. "Can we call him?"

"This is ridiculous," Marcus said, shaking his fist still gripping the cell phone. "We're wasting time—we should be calling the police!"

Raiden looked at Elle, who was looking back at him, waiting for him to tell them what to do.

"Fine," he sighed. "Call the police."

Marcus started to dial when Elle cried out. "Wait! Is that them?"

Raiden turned around to see Jason and Logan walking hand in hand up the sidewalk.

Eleven

Elle brushed Raiden's arm as she ran past him.

"Where the hell were you?" she asked, pulling Logan into her arms.

"We weren't sure how long you guys would be, so we decided to walk around the block," said Jason, looking at them all in confusion. "What's the big deal?"

"I had no idea where you went." Elle squeezed Logan even harder.

"Mommy," Logan groaned into her chest, "you're squishing me."

"Thank God you're all right," she said, releasing him. Raiden was standing next to them.

"Wait," Jason said, his brows climbing higher.

"You didn't think—did you actually think I kidnapped my own son?"

Elle stood to look Jason in the eyes but maintained a tight grip on Logan's hand.

"I came out here and you were both gone," she said. "What was I supposed to think?"

"You have my cell number. You could have just called me."

"I deleted it," she said, and Jason's face fell.

"You deleted it?"

"Last year. It's not like you ever called us." Elle brushed a stray hair from her face.

Marcus came over and took Logan's hand from hers. "Logan, what do you say we go inside and make some lunch?"

He nodded and followed his papa to the front door.

"The point is," said Raiden when they were out of earshot, "that you can't just walk off with Logan without saying something to us."

Jason's expression turned to venom as he glared at Raiden. "You stay out of this. He's not your son."

"He's not your son either," Elle spat back, and both men looked at her in surprise.

"What—what are you trying to say?" Jason asked.

"Not that," she said, rolling her eyes.

"Biologically, of course he's yours. Logan's a carbon copy of you, for Christ's sake. But you stopped being his father the day you walked out on us. The only reason you still have any right to him is because I kept hoping in vain that you would come back."

"I'm here now," Jason said, and Raiden sucked in a breath.

"It's too late," Elle told him. "A real father, a real husband, doesn't take two fucking years to decide he wants to be a part of his own family."

"So that's it then?" Jason asked.

"Yes. That's it," Elle said and crossed her arms. "Good luck ever seeing your son again."

"Hold on," Raiden said, and he dragged Elle away from Jason.

"What are you doing? Let go of me," she yelled, wrenching her arm from his grip.

"You're too angry right now," he told her.

"Of course I'm angry."

"You need to think about this before you start making decisions."

"What is there to think about? Jason's a deadbeat dad and now he's trying to worm his way back into our lives. I don't ever want to see him again."

"I don't blame you," he said, looking up at the house. "But you need to keep in mind who else is involved in this. And what's best for everyone."

Elle followed his gaze to the window, where Logan was peeking out from behind the curtains, smiling and waving. "Are you saying I should give him what he wants?" she asked, turning back to Raiden.

"I'm not telling you what to do. I'll stand behind whatever decision you make. But you should think about the long term, about the pros and cons before you make that decision."

She pressed her palms to her forehead; she could feel a headache coming on.

"What if," Raiden started, and Elle dropped her hands to look at him again, "I tell him to come back later today? Give you some time to think about it."

Elle didn't want to think about it. She wanted to tell Jason to just go away and let them all pretend that he hadn't shown up on her doorstep just as things were going really well for her.

But Raiden was right—there was Logan to consider.

"Fine," she said. "But I can't promise I'll change my mind."

"I understand. And I support whatever you decide to do."

Raiden walked back to where Jason was standing on the sidewalk, and Elle stared at her feet.

"She can't do this, I'll fight—" Elle heard Jason say, but Raiden's words cut him off. She couldn't quite make out what he was saying—not that it mattered. As a lawyer, she trusted Raiden was being very diplomatic with his words.

When she heard car beep, Elle finally dared to look up and watched Jason get into his car, fuming as he slammed the door and drove away.

"What did he say?" she asked as she and Raiden headed to the house.

"He'll be back in two hours."

There was a knock at the door exactly two hours later, and Elle gave Raiden a nervous glance as she walked over to answer it.

"You've got this," he reassured her, giving a nod.

Jason said nothing when she opened the door, he just stood there with puppy dog eyes.

"You need to find a lawyer," she told him, wanting to get this over with as quickly as possible.

"That's it, then. You really are going to keep Logan from me."

"No, I'm not," she said, shaking her head. "Raiden was right. I love him too much to do that. You need a lawyer because this divorce is happening. We will agree to a custody plan."

He nodded, and Elle handed him a business card.

"This is who will be representing me."

Jason sighed as he took it.

"Please don't drag this out," she said. "It doesn't need to be any harder than it already is."

"I understand."

"Here's your bag." She picked up the duffel she'd left by the door after rounding up the couple of things he had pulled out.

"Can I at least say goodbye to Logan?"

"Of course."

Elle called Logan over and he hugged Jason, who looked reluctant to let their son go.

"When will you come back?" Logan asked, and Elle knew she had made the right choice in not denying him his father.

"Soon," Jason said, looking up at Elle, who nodded. "I promise."

Logan seemed satisfied with that response. "Okay," he said and ran back off into the other room.

"Bye," she said, handing Jason the bag.

He took it. "I'll be in touch soon," he said, holding up the card.

Elle slowly closed the door behind him and pressed her forehead against it.

"Are you okay?" Raiden asked from behind her.

She mustered a smile and nodded. "I will be."

Even though it had been a false alarm, Raiden couldn't help noticing that Elle stayed by Logan's side for the rest of the day, barely taking her eyes off of him. He waited patiently outside Logan's room that night, listening to her read him another bedtime story. He could just as easily have waited downstairs, or in Elle's room even, but he liked hearing their voices through the crack in the door. It had hurt when Jason made the comment about Logan not being his son, but the truth in that statement didn't change how he felt about that kid.

Raiden heard the bed creak and he backed up to the opposite wall as Elle stepped out, gently closing the door behind her.

"He's finally asleep," she said. "He has no idea."

Raiden frowned, not understanding what she meant.

"I thought I was going to lose him," she said, pressing a cheek against Raiden's chest, and he wrapped his arms around her. "For a split second, I honestly thought Jason had run away with him and I would never see him again."

"I'm so sorry," Raiden murmured, resting his chin on top of her head.

Elle pulled away. "What are you sorry for? You're not the one who walked off with my son without talking to me first. I know you would never do that to me."

"Because if I hadn't encouraged you to send the divorce papers, Jason wouldn't have come running out here. This never would have happened."

"I told you, Raiden, this was something that I should have done a long time ago."

He shrugged. "I still can't help feeling responsible for this somehow. That you should be just as angry with me as you are with Jason."

Elle shook her head, frowning. "I am nothing but grateful for having you in my life."

Raiden thumbed her cheek. "When I walked out the door yesterday, I thought I was going to lose you," he said. "You and Logan both. And I didn't know if I could bear it."

"I'm so sorry," she replied. "Jason coming back caught me off guard, and after dreaming about it for so long...."

"It's okay," he told her. "I get it."

"I'm sorry," she repeated. "I love you."

"I know," he said and started to lean in for a kiss, but she stopped him.

"No, I mean I *love* you. I don't want to wake up and ever have you not be there."

"And you won't. I promise."

"I know," she said. "I mean, I believe you. And

that's why I want you to move in with us."

"Really?"

She nodded.

Raiden started to kiss her but pulled away.

"You're really sure this is what you want?" he asked.

"Without a doubt," she said and lifted her lips to his.

Elle felt nauseous as she stepped off the elevator three weeks later into her father's firm.

"Elle."

She turned to see Raiden coming down the hall. Just the sight of him helped ease some of her nervousness.

"How're you doing?" he asked.

"I feel like I'm going to be sick," she said.

"It'll be fine," he said, rubbing her arm. "You don't think he's going to contest anything, do you?"

"Not really. But everything's moving so quickly, I keep waiting for it all to blow up in my face."

"We'll deal with it together if it does." He gave her hand a gentle squeeze.

"Thank you," she said with a small smile.

"Ms. Peyton?"

Raiden and Elle looked up to see Diana Lee, Elle's divorce lawyer, standing in the doorway of one of the conference rooms.

"Whenever you're ready," she said.

Elle took one last look at Raiden.

"Good luck," he said, giving her a kiss on the cheek. "I'll see you when it's all over."

She nodded and walked over to the conference room. Inside, she sat at the table across from Jason and his lawyer, Erick Jones.

After pleasantries were exchanged, they got right down to business, and Elle wondered why she had been so worried. Neither one of them was asking for much, and the only major asset to be split up was the house.

"My client will be putting it on the market as soon as possible," said Diana, "and has agreed to share half the proceeds of the sale."

"You don't have to sell it," Jason cut in. "I'm okay with signing over my half of it."

"It's all right," Elle told him. "I'm planning to sell it anyway."

"But where will you and Logan live?" Jason asked with a frown.

Elle squirmed in her seat before answering.

"Raiden and I are planning to buy a house together," she finally said.

"Oh."

"So we're agreed on selling the house and

splitting it?" Diana asked, looking around the table. Nobody argued. "I'll take that as a yes, then."

"Now onto the custody plan," Jason's lawyer said, shuffling some papers. "My client agrees to the terms, so if there are no more questions…."

"I have one more thing I would like to add," Elle said, her heart pounding, and everyone looked at her in alarm. "I need Jason to understand how important this is. That if you back out of it, or if you *ever* run off again—"

"I won't," Jason said, sitting up straight.

"—then it's over. And you never get to see Logan again."

"Ms. Peyton!" Erick barked.

"No, it's alright," Jason said, holding up a hand to silence him.

Elle looked Jason right in the eye. "I won't have you coming in and out of his life."

"I understand. And I won't." Jason turned to his lawyer. "I agree to the clause. She's absolutely right."

Erick scowled as he made a note on his papers.

Elle breathed a quiet sigh of relief. It had only occurred to her this morning to make the request, but she hadn't been sure how Jason would react. She only hoped he was serious about understanding.

After another tedious hour, everything was

properly initialed and signed. All that was left now was to wait for the official date.

"So that's it?" Jason asked as everyone stood.

Elle nodded.

"Do you want to grab coffee or something?"

"I don't think that's a good idea," she said.

"Oh. Yeah, sure."

"But you should come over this weekend and hang out with Logan."

His face lit up. "That would be great!"

"Have you found a place yet?" she asked as they walked out of the conference room and toward the elevators.

"I did. I move in on the first of next month. It's right by my new job, so I feel pretty fortunate."

"Good," she said.

"Are you going down as well?" Jason asked as he pushed the button for the elevator.

"No. I, uh…." She pointed over her shoulder. "No," she said, dropping her hand.

"Right. Raiden."

Elle smiled weakly at him.

"I guess I'll see you this weekend then," he said and stepped into the elevator.

She gave him a nod and waited for the doors to close before walking down the hall to Raiden's office. No one was there. She headed back down the hall and ran into Cassie.

"Have you seen Raiden?" asked Elle.

"Yeah! He told me to tell you that he had an emergency and had to run off. He said he would meet you at your house later."

"I see," Elle said, frowning.

"So how did it go?" Cassie asked.

"It went well. Everything is signed and being filed as we speak."

"Good. That's good to hear."

A phone on Cassie's desk started ringing.

"Oops, gotta go!" she said and rushed off.

Once on the road, Elle decided to take a little detour before heading home. Jeannie had taken Logan for the day in case things didn't go well and she had no idea how long Raiden's emergency would be, so why not?

Elle pulled up in front of a house less than a mile from her home. Two weeks ago she and Raiden had been out for a walk with Logan when they stumbled upon a realtor's open house. She and Raiden were immediately in love with the Tudor-style home. It was only slightly bigger than her current home but boasted a generous backyard—one she could imagine Logan running around in. Problem was there was no point applying for a home loan until her divorce was final, and she knew there was no way a gem like this would stay on the market for that long. She glanced at the for-sale sign and knew she had been right—there was a sold sign slashed across it. Oh well, there were sure to be other dream homes available when they were ready.

The disappointment sitting in the pit of her stomach disappeared when she saw Raiden's car parked on her street.

He greeted her at the door when she walked in.

"How did it go?" he asked.

"Good. Now we just wait."

Raiden pulled her into his arms.

"How do you feel?" he asked.

At first she thought it was an odd question, but in trying to answer it, she understood.

"I feel…weird," she said. "Glad that it's over. Also sad that it's over."

He nodded slowly.

"Is that how you felt?" she asked.

"Yes. Let's focus on the glad part right now, though." He took her hand and pulled her toward the kitchen, where she noticed a bottle of champagne. "We should celebrate."

Elle laughed. "Are we celebrating that you aren't sleeping with a married woman anymore?"

"I never was," he said as he filled two glasses.

"Maybe on paper you were, but that was no marriage." He handed her a glass and held his up. "Here's to new beginnings."

"I can drink to that. Cheers!" They clinked glasses and she took a sip.

"And to this," he said, pulling a piece of paper from his back pocket and handing it to her.

"What's this?" Elle set down her glass and unfolded it. It was a flyer for the Tudor house, and her heart sank.

"But it's too late," she said. "I just drove by it on my way home and it already sold."

"I know," he said with a smirk. "That's because I bought it."

"What? But how—why?"

"We both knew it was perfect for us, even if the timing wasn't. I had enough for the down payment and figured you can always add your name to the loan when you're ready."

"Oh my God," Elle whispered, looking the flyer again, then back to Raiden. "You did this? For me?"

"For us," he said. "There is one condition to you putting your name on the paperwork, though,"

"Of course," she answered, knowing that Raiden was a lawyer after all.

But then he surprised her by getting down on one knee and pulling something else from his pocket.

"Marry me, Elle," he said, opening a black velvet box to reveal a diamond ring. Elle's eyes went big and her heart raced. "Let me show you and Logan what it means to be a family."

Elle could feel the tears welling up in her eyes. "Yes," she said quietly as she kneeled before him. "Yes, I want to marry you."

Raiden put the ring on her finger. "I love you, Elle."

"I love you," she said and kissed him.

Epilogue

The sky was still gray when Logan came bounding into their bedroom.

"Mommy, Raiden, wake up! I get to go to school today!"

Elle rubbed the sleep from her eyes and felt Raiden rousing next to her.

"Sweetie, we don't leave for another," she glanced at the clock, "two hours. You should still be sleeping."

"But I'm too excited!" he said with the biggest grin on his face.

Elle sighed. She still couldn't believe her little man was starting kindergarten today.

"I know," she said, sitting up. "I just need a

couple more minutes to wake up. Wait for me downstairs, and then I'll make you a special first day of school breakfast."

Logan squealed as he ran out of the room.

"Someone's excited," Raiden said from beside her.

"It's a big day for him," she said with a smile. "I just hope Jason remembers to be there on time."

"He's been doing a good job sticking to the plan."

"I know. But every visit or big event, I get nervous he's going to flake out."

"And if that day comes, we'll deal with it then."

She nodded.

"You know…." He started caressing her back. "There's something else special about today."

She lay back down facing him. "You think I don't know, don't you?"

He grinned. "I think you do know."

"Happy six-month anniversary," she said, giving him a kiss.

"Happy six-month anniversary, Mrs. Kane. I even got you something."

"You did?"

"Nothing big, but you have to wait until dinner tonight."

She frowned. "You're such a tease. But that's

okay, because I have a surprise for you, but I can't wait until tonight. I think I'll burst if I don't tell you soon."

"And what surprise could that be?"

She turned to her bedside table and pulled a box from the drawer before facing him again.

"Is this a watch?" he asked, looking down at the long, slender box.

"Better," she said, buzzing with anticipation.

He carefully lifted the lid and found a pregnancy stick in it. He looked at Elle, back at the stick, and then back to her.

"Does this mean what I think it means?" he asked.

She nodded.

"But I thought you said it could take a couple months after going off the pill?"

"'Could' being the operative word," she said. "Looks like first time's the charm for us."

His face finally broke into the grin she'd been waiting for.

"We're having a baby," he whispered, still looking at the box.

She nodded again, and then to her dismay, his grin began to fade.

"What's wrong?" she asked.

He looked up at her with worry in his eyes. "Do

you think I'll make a good father?"

"Are you serious? I don't think," she said, "I *know* you'll make an amazing dad. Look at you and Logan."

"But don't you worry this will be different?" he asked.

"No," she said confidently. "You have this insane capacity to love. Look at the way you've taken care of your mom. And the way you take care of Logan and me."

He nodded, his expression softening, and Elle could see her words sinking into him.

"I'm going to be a father," he said, the smile slowly returning. "Some little guy is gonna call me daddy. Or girl. Do we know what it is?"

"It's too soon," she said, shaking her head. "I only just found out two days ago and decided to wait for today. We won't find out the sex for another couple months."

"Who cares, we're having a baby!"

"Of course I am. It's perfect. You, Logan," he placed a hand on her belly, "and our baby—this is all absolutely perfect."

Also by Alex Strong

Island Runaway
CrossFire
No Way Out
Ghost Lies

Gratitude

I want to thank my friend Cattigan as always for being my beta-reader and all the help you do in general. My books are better and I am more successful because of you.

Huge props to my editor Carrie for the amazing work you have done on this. It is always a pleasure working with you and I feel more confident putting this book out there knowing that you have gone over it. I look forward to the next project together.

I would like to applaud my friends for putting up with me through all this and for patiently listening to my crazy ideas and my grips about word counts and formatting.

And thank you to my husband for being as supportive as always and to my kids for being understanding when I'm off in another world, even if I'm sitting right next to them.

I also need to give a shout out to all the awesome readers for taking the time to read what I have written. At the risk of sounding cheesy, or at least like a flight attendant, I know you have a choice, and thank you for choosing me.

Alex Strong has loved stories, whether she's reading them or telling them, since she was very young. But it wasn't until after the birth of her youngest son that she realized how much she wanted to be an author. Her past lives include working as a waitress, a sales clerk, and a nanny. She has been all around the world including two years living in the Philippines as child. She is now proud to call the Pacific Northwest her home and currently lives in the Seattle suburbs with her family and their two dogs.

www.ingramcontent.com/pod-product-compliance
Lightning Source LLC
Chambersburg PA
CBHW070822120626

46556CB00002B/627